GRYPHON BOOKS
3

Winners
and Losers

GRYPHON BOOKS
General Editor Rhodri Jones

Michael A. Pearson

Winners
and Losers

JOHN MURRAY

Copyright © 1984 Michael A. Pearson

First published 1984 by Methuen Children's Books Ltd

Published in *Gryphon Books* 1988 by
John Murray (Publishers) Ltd
50 Albemarle Street
London W1X 4BD

British Library Cataloguing in Publication Data

Pearson, Michael A.
  Winners and losers.—(Gryphon books; 3)
  I. Title   II. Series
  823'.914[J]   PZ7
  ISBN 0-7195-4509-9

Typeset in 11/13pt Sabon
by Inforum Ltd, Portsmouth
Printed and bound in Great Britain
by Biddles of Guildford

Contents

The Fool and the Fairy Tale

All was quiet in the library. It had to be. We'd just had a second warning from Mrs Potter. She didn't give us any details either, which was a bad sign; just the words 'The next person who talks or makes a noise . . . will regret it!'

The silence was heavy as 3L bent low over their books, twenty-five kids each imagining a different kind of punishment. But the sacred hush of the library was broken sooner than even we expected.

'Yer! Eh! Wanna see my clockwork Womble?' a voice whispered across the table.

The large pair of spectacles opposite me flashed and twinkled as Benny looked up from his book. Behind his left shoulder I could see Mrs P. glance up sharply as her bat's ears detected sound bouncing off the ceiling.

I shook my head slightly. It wasn't worth the trouble. Besides I'd seen his stupid Womble in break. It was three inches high and moved like an old man wading through thick mud. It also made a lot of noise.

Suddenly my neighbour, Gary Streeter, nudged me.

'Yeah, go on then, Ben,' he whispered. 'Send it across!'

I winced as the winding mechanism chirruped like a cricket. Benny put the clockwork Womble on the table top, about to send it across no-man's land from his baby-reader to my history of the American Civil War. Then he had second thoughts and went underground. He disappeared from sight and placed the Womble on the floor ready to march him off under the table to my feet.

'Benny Mcmenemy, sit up!'

He sat up; like a ticket in a till. But the look on his face told us he'd already set the toy in motion. Typical Benny though, he'd put it down back to front, so instead of waddling its uneasy way under cover, it was heading out through the legs of Benny's chair — straight across the open library floor!

There was nothing any of us could do, except watch the big showdown. The library went even more quiet, but with the total silence of everybody listening to a strange sound, like sand being poured endlessly into a metal tray. Everyone looked up and round to try and identify it. Mrs Potter jerked her head slightly as if some wasp had buzzed too close to her ear. Then, as the class continued to stretch and scrape to get a glimpse of this unknown hero who dared break the sacred silence of library lesson, she leapt up, eyes wide with surprise, brows knit with annoyance.

Yes, Mrs Potter, there is a funny whirring noise coming from our table. And, oh yes, Mrs Potter, that squat little object strolling bravely from under Benny's chair is indeed the culprit.

Great Uncle Bulgaria was going great guns until Mrs Potter swooped and snatched him off his plastic feet. He kicked his legs feebly to escape as the class tittered and giggled.

'Whose, and what is this?' she asked gently with a menacing smile.

Benny, who at least is an honest fool, stood straight up and announced, almost proudly: 'Ooh, that's my clock-work Womble, sir — miss!'

The toy was confiscated. The boy was kicked out and spent the rest of the lesson outside the classroom door. At least that's where we all thought he was.

Then, just five minutes before the bell went, the door flew open and in strode Mr Smart, the humanities teacher with his thumb and forefinger clamped on to Benny's pink ear. Smart could be a real swine sometimes.

'This one of your lost lambs, Mrs Potter?' he roared joyfully, giving Benny's blond head a quick shake. 'Strayed from your flock, I fancy. Thought he'd pop in to watch one of our fourth year humanities films, yes. Didn't spot him at first in the dark there. Then I wondered why the class's I.Q. had dropped suddenly.'

Now this was obviously a teacher's joke and the two teachers gave each other a knowing smirk, but because it was Benny the whole class had a good laugh too.

It was all typical Benny. Trouble followed him like a shadow; a great bullying shadow pushing him into one scrape after the other, and never letting him escape. Mind you, he asked for it. He was always trying to prove he was something special. He was one of those kids who tries so hard that he always ends up proving he's nothing but a fool: like showing off to first year tots with Kung-Fu kicks that threw him flat on his back, or wearing such high heeled shoes that he was forever falling over.

I suppose his hare-lip might have had something to do

3

with it, making him a sort of constant odd-bod, but I don't know . . .

Anyway what did worry me soon after the library incident was the way Benny started to follow me around all over the place. I couldn't think why he was, perhaps because I'd helped him finish his English homework in break. Talk about hieroglyphics! After I'd deciphered the first five lines I found out it was a silly fairy tale about mushrooms and how the sun made them pop out of the ground. Load of rubbish of course, but when Mrs Potter handed it back she put on the bottom of his story: 'A fascinating and nicely written story, Benny. Well done.' God, was he chuffed! Once I'd explained to him what 'fascinating' meant.

As I walked home that Wednesday evening, filling my lungs with fresh air after the stench of school, I heard this lispy voice calling my name. It was Benny of course, still flushed with triumph at the first decent mark he'd ever had in English. (Well, he didn't actually see any mark, she kept those for her little blue book.)

'Keep walking,' I told myself with gritted teeth. The Sharpness coach was coming out of the main gate and was due past any second with all the hardnuts on board, and I didn't want them to see me walking with him.

'Here, what's running for? Hold on,' he gasped, panting along behind me. 'I got something for you. Honest!'

It was a trick of course, but I fell for it and slowed down. 'Here,' he said, beaming at me, his glasses twinkling and flashing in the autumn sun. 'How'd you like more mushrooms than you could eat, eh? You likes mushrooms, don't you?'

I just shook my head and kept going. I couldn't stand the taste of them. But wait a minute, I thought, hang on. I didn't like mushrooms, no, but I knew somebody who did; my Aunty Agnes was wild about them.

She was from Canada. She'd gone there twenty years ago and was back in England again for a couple of weeks holiday. She was really nice, full of funny stories, nice presents, telling us how marvellous Canada was. And she was hellova rich! Only yesterday I'd heard her say to Mum how she'd love to taste some Severnside mushrooms again. Benny's offer now sounded quite tempting.

'Meet me at seven o'clock tomorrow morning, all right?' he invited eagerly. 'Outside the kennels, O.K.?'

Seven o'clock? I hadn't got up that early since my paper round. And the kennels were miles away; the other side of town.

'Has to be early morning,' he said, becoming the expert all of a sudden. 'It's the mornin' sun brings 'em up, see?'

I remembered his story and it still sounded like a fairy tale; you know, the sun rises and all these little mushrooms pop out of the ground on springs? Still, I'd only been living in the country for eighteen months so perhaps there were some things I didn't know about.

Next morning with help from Mum, who knew of my secret mission, I just managed to be outside the hunt kennels at seven o'clock. It was still quite dark. I stumbled sleepily towards the waiting Benny, carrying my empty bag and shivering in the cold grey air.

'Follow me,' he called, waving me after him like I was the last of the Mohicans.

5

We walked past the common and came to this flat field which I knew belonged to old farmer Pritchard. He came in the pub now and then, usually after parents' evenings, because his son was in the fourth year. He was a fat, red-faced Welshman; short, with beady blue eyes. He spent his time herding cows into his fields and chasing kids out of them. When he wasn't chasing after foxes with the rest of the hunt, that is.

When we got there, and reached the gate, Benny climbs on top and just sits there, like some blond, bespectacled leprechaun.

'Hey, what are you waiting for?' I yelled out, feeling pretty cold by now.

'Sun'll be up in a minute,' he whispered as if the sun was hiding behind the next hedgerow listening. I leaned against the gate, while he acted out his little fairy tale, and kept an eye open for Pritchard.

Then suddenly Benny turned to me, put his fingers to his lips and pointed across the field. At first I couldn't see what he meant, but then slowly it all began to happen.

Dark lurking hedgerows began to glow sort of golden. I looked up at the sky lightening to blue, and glanced around me, almost in alarm. Hills in the distance were blue and purple with pink clouds floating over them. Two ragged crows rose from the elm wood and flapped lazily away, off across the fields towards the river. The whole countryside was coming to life. You could hear it shifting and singing to itself like an enormous, invisible creature awakening.

Benny just sat on his gate, listening and watching over his fairy-tale landscape full of a kind of confidence that made me feel like a fool. In the gap at the corner of the field, this band of gold began to spread across.

'Now, you look. They're coming up! There! See!'

I stood and watched spellbound. Following his pointing arm I saw at first one, then two, then several, whitish pin-points of light amid the greyish carpets of lush grass. Some were moored to the grass with yellowy cobwebs. But suddenly there was a whole galaxy of white points; more with every second until the field was full. Full of mushrooms.

Benny gave a great whoop and clutching his paper bags leapt into the field and began to pick them, fast and furiously.

I had my own bag full and bulging in no time and I sat back on my haunches in the damp, dew-necklaced grass. In the distance I could hear some cows mooing, which meant Pritchard was somewhere around. Then a sudden thought chilled me to the marrow.

'Here, Benny, how d'you know they aren't . . . poisonous?'

'Rubbish! They ain't poisonous!' he laughed, filling his third bag.

'Ah, but how d'you know for sure, I mean? I wouldn't know, see, I'm still a bit of a townie.'

'They ain't poisonous, 'cos they ain't that's why!'

I got slowly to my feet. I had a bagful of these mushrooms, but didn't know whether they were really safe or not. I mean it was no good bringing Aunty Agnes her mushrooms and feeling angelic about it, if we had to send her back to Canada in a coffin. I suppose I'd have to take his word for it. But just as I was ready to go, a voice bellowed at us from the gate.

'You kids! Stop that! Don't pick they mushrooms, d'you hear?'

I spun round and saw this fat little bloke in thick coat and trilby hat come waddling towards us, a bit like Benny's clockwork Womble. His eyes were twinkling.

At first I thought of making a run for it, but something in the tone of his voice made me stop still.

'Here, you haven't eaten none of they mushrooms, have you, kid?' he rasped, all wide-eyed with worry. I shook my head.

Pritchard rushed up to Benny who was still on his knees, grabbed him fiercely and pulled him away.

'What's the matter with 'ee, kid? D'you hear what I said? You haven't eaten none of they mushrooms have you? I'll have to put me finger down yer throat if you have.'

He held Benny's face by the chin and tried to get his fat little finger into his fat little mouth.

'Here,' I gasped, as they struggled among the mushrooms. 'Are they poisonous or something?'

'Poisonous?' he growled at me. 'Poisonous indeed? These be rare mushrooms, these be. Why, if you've eaten any, you've got ten seconds of life left. I'll have to put me finger down yer throat.'

Well that did it. I threw my bag open, swung it upside down and tipped its contents on to the grass. As Benny broke away from Pritchard I clouted the kid with it.

'Get moving,' I snarled nastily. 'Go on, you mongo!'

'You're lucky I caught you at it, indeed. You'd best be on your way, lads!' Pritchard called quite kindly after us, yet with a sort of triumphant note in his voice as well.

I kicked and clouted Benny to the gate and over it, as he blubbered it wasn't true and the mushrooms were all right, and that. I wondered how many years' probation I'd have got for poisoning Aunty Agnes.

Benny was pretty upset of course, sniffling and red-faced and struggling with himself as he walked away. Then he turned and started to run back to the field.

'Where the hell are you off to, nutcase?' I shouted.

'Gonna get me paper bags back,' he sobbed, waving me away.

I went back after him. How pathetic can you get, I thought.

But as he climbed the gate he froze.

'You come here, Ducker! You flippin' take a look at this!'

I climbed up beside him wondering what other fairy-tale landscape he could see. All I could see was Pritchard squatting on the grass, the most evil smile on his red face shovelling all the 'poisonous mushrooms' into our own bags and stuffing them into his pockets.

'He's pinching our mushrooms!' screamed Benny loudly. 'I told you they wasn't poisonous, Ducker! I'll Kung-Fu 'im, I will.'

I'd felt angry before, but now I was speechless. I just stood there. At that point Pritchard saw us.

'You two, get off that bleedin' gate! Get you home!'

'Never mind your gate!' Benny shouted. 'What about our bloody mushrooms!'

And as I watched, he leapt into the field in a valiant effort to retrieve them. But his Kung-Fu kick missed by

9

miles. Pritchard gave him one clout across the head and Benny was running back to the gate.

I didn't know what to say to him on the way home, past the common and the hunt kennels. In the end I just patted his shoulder.

'Sorry, Benny. I didn't believe you!'

Instead of being angry or sarcastic, his face lit up for a moment, like I'd said something good about him. Then he frowned.

'Don't tell none of the others about this lark, mind.'

'Why not?' I asked puzzled. 'Wasn't your fault. I didn't know that Pritchard was such a crafty bastard.'

'I know,' he said mysteriously. 'But they wouldn't see it that way.'

He looked away and tugged a leaf off the hedge we were passing. The sad thing was, I knew he was right.

The Season of Goodwill

The bell rang for morning break. As the teacher rushed off for his morning coffee and the class got noisily to its feet, I reached eagerly into my jacket pocket ready for the eleven o'clock ritual.

I took out the colourful packet of bubble gum, gripped the twirls of paper at either end and pulled gently. The twirls stretched and straightened out and with a soft crackle of paper the powdery, pink tongue of bubble gum broke out in a delicious smile. I paused and sniffed delicately, staring upwards at nothing in particular.

My nostrils twitched with the sugary fruity smell that only bubble gum has. Without further delay, I popped it into my mouth and chewed. The lump of sweet lead became softer and softer and fleshy until it was like a sort of sugary mussel.

'Chewing in class, lad?' barked this harsh voice behind me, shattering my moment of bliss. It was Braddock's voice; Braddock, the sports master and deadly gum-hunter. 'Go on then, spit it out!'

Already visualising the raised arm and open hand, I instinctively spat the treasured pink blob right into the bin at my feet. As it clanged metallically there was a loud, uncontrollable snigger behind me.

I spun round, red in the face with fury. It wasn't Braddock.

'Fooled you that time, sucker!' shrieked Jammy, killing himself with triumphant laughter. Jammy was of course very good at impressions; TV actors, pop stars, teachers. Braddock was his party piece. And I was livid.

'You swine! That was a fresh one. That's one fresh bubbly you owe me!'

He took a sharp step backwards, thinking I was going to hit him. But then he realised I wasn't the striking kind and relaxed.

'O.K. hardnut,' he answered smiling, the colour returning to his white face. 'If you're a good boy in drama, I'll bring you one tomorrow.'

I nodded, but not out of gratitude. Judging by the big white Mercedes his dad drove, Jammy could afford to bring me ten fresh bubblies.

Julian Armstrong-Mayes had come to our school two weeks after the start of the Autumn term, which was typical. He was a tall thin kid with carefully permed blond hair and dark beady eyes that didn't seem to fit. He was a weird character really. Posh with the teachers, but normal with us lot. Sometimes too normal. He always had this cheeky dimpled smile on his face, and right from the beginning he set himself up as my big rival.

For a start he seemed to be very brainy; far cleverer than the others in the class and nearly as clever as me. But where he had the edge on me all the way was in drama lessons. He was a brilliant actor. And the girls thought he was fantastic, naturally, all falling at his feet from the very first day. He seemed to walk on a carpet of swooning girls. He didn't look anything like Robert Redford, if you ask me.

Even Jacky, whose tiger-grey eyes were once for me only, had joined the soppy mob of females drooling over him. It was a good job I spotted his initials spelt out J-A-M, otherwise we'd never have been able to cut him down to size.

Well, his latest triumph in drama lessons was getting the main part in this Nativity play we were going to do at Christmas in front of the whole school. It was a funny business, when I look back on it.

We'd never done any Nativity plays in the first two years; our drama teacher, Miss Silverberg, wasn't all that keen on them for some reason. But in the first term of the third year, we had this new teacher (well, actually, Miss Gardeno was a student, only we weren't supposed to know that) and she took us for a double period each week. She was really good looking too; tall, long red hair, lovely pink face and sparkling blue eyes. Me and the lads would do anything for her. Our behaviour was immaculate; our manners were finer than the Duke of Edinburgh's.

Now everyone knows that the Nativity play's all about Joseph and Mary going to the inn and all that, with baby Jesus, and everything's full up so they have to spend the night in a stable? Well, Miss Gardeno has modernised the whole thing. There were Joe and Mary driving their car and it breaks down so they go to this motel which is full up and so on. Instead of shepherds abiding in the fields, we had miners coming off the night shift. They had to do their bit all together, which was tricky, I can tell you.

Instead of the three wise men, we had three professors; an Indian physicist, an African biologist and a Scottish chemist. Everything was brought up to date. Well, anyway, it made a change. And besides, Miss Gardeno had chosen our class to do it in front of the whole school, which was quite an honour, I suppose.

Jammy played the part of Joseph; but the innkeeper, the motel-owner, I mean, who is a nasty character, very rude and lucky not to get struck down by a thunderbolt considering who he's talking to, well, that was my part. Two sentences. I had to be very rich, snobbish and smoke a long cigar. No, only a dummy cigar, made out of rolled brown cloth which smouldered and tasted so horrible they were lucky I didn't throw up.

Jacky was Mary, and that part annoyed me most of all. I suppose with her long brown hair she was the best choice, but she's pretty good at acting herself, and the way she made eyes at Joseph I never knew if it was real or put on. To tell you the truth she'd been acting pretty strangely ever since this Miss Gardeno arrived.

There's one thing about Jammy that I haven't mentioned; his mucking about! He's good at acting and that, but his trouble is he doesn't know when to stop and, unlike me, he doesn't know how to stay out of trouble. He really used to get on Mrs Potter's nerves in English. I've never seen her so livid. 'I think, Julian, that you had better get out of my sight!' just before she chucks him out into the corridor.

Braddock used to dap him every lesson, twice, and

sometimes in between. But Jammy saved most of his ideas up for drama and Miss Gardeno; because she wasn't a real teacher, I suppose. Of course the rest of the class used to love it when he played her up, especially the girls. We would all sit back and watch the three-act comedy: One, he mucks about, Two, she loses her temper, Three he cops it. Every lesson that is. But because he was so good in drama at the same time, you could see she didn't like to chuck him out of the lesson. Even in the rehearsals of this play he was mucking about like crazy.

We had about a week to go until the real performance. It was pretty important too, doing it in front of the headmaster, teachers and any parents who chose to wander in. But that dinner hour everything was going wrong. Miss G. was getting more and more mad at us. She was pretty excitable at the best of times. So, it's scene one and here's Joe and Mary coming up to the motel. I'm waiting behind the curtains for my cue. A knock on the knocker, off-stage, of course.

'Hullo, hullo, hullo,' I hear Jammy say, 'Is there any-body in the inn? Come out of the inn!'

I could tell he was a fooling around again. The knocker goes and I poke my head out of the curtains.

'And what do you want, my man?' I snarl at them in a posh sort of voice. 'Ah, Innkeeper, how can you keep'er out? How can yer keep'er outside waiting in the cold, cold night? She is with child and wants a room and all that. Have you a room within the inn, or without the inn; but not without the innkeeper's permission.'

'JULIAN!' Miss Gardeno shrieked, blue eyes blazing, red hair lashing about. 'This is your last warning. If you don't stop fooling around I shall take the part away from you and give it to someone else.'

We did the scene again, and this time it all went smoothly, because he had to call me 'motel manager', and he hadn't thought up any stupid jokes to go with that. You see, we didn't use scripts or anything; we had to make it up as we went along, which was more fun, if you were in the mood, but useless if you had someone like Jammy about, all ready to start cracking the jokes.

He did behave himself very well for the rest of that rehearsal and Miss G. praised him for it. But come the dress rehearsal and he's worse than ever.

It's scene one again and I'm in full costume this time: black jacket and trousers, bow tie and fancy waistcoat (borrowed from Jammy actually), black moustache, which keeps coming off and that awful smelly cigar. Enter Joe and Mary. A knock at the knocker.

'Yes? What do you two want?' I snarl nastily at them. 'It's gone two o'clock.'

'My good woman and I,' Jammy begins, 'do humbly beseech thee to let us poor, deprived ones partake of your bountiful amenities, if thou wilt?'

Oh no, here we go again, I think to myself. It's no good, I can't help it. The sniggers and giggles start spurting out of me. I'm so busy shaking and laughing and trying to keep a straight face, I haven't a clue what to say next. Jammy stepped forward to plug the gap in the play.

'Look here, my good man. Tut, tut, I see no cause for mirth. Come on then, let us in this dump.'

That last bit did it I suppose. Suddenly Miss Gardeno appears among us on stage, Jammy promptly disappears, muttering horrible threats over his breath, promising revenge on us all.

True to her word she took the part away from him. But she did the worst possible thing. She gave it to me and made him the motel owner. If he could make me laugh once, what was stopping him from doing it again? Yet, strangely enough a sudden change had come over him. He began to act very seriously and normally, at last. It was as if he'd learnt his lesson. I guessed he was hoping to get that part back in the last minute.

I'm not bad at acting, but I'm no Laurence Olivier. What worried me was the thought of leaping from a ten word part to one of the leads. It worried me so much that on the day of the big performance I felt this icy stalagmite in my stomach growing taller and taller until it was tickling the back of my throat.

My beloved spouse was no help either. At every opportunity she'd come up to me, punch me in the gut and say, 'Well? D'you know what you got to say? D'you know it all? You aren't going to forget it or get anything wrong again, are you?'

I kept trying to remember Miss Gardeno's advice. 'It isn't what you say, as long as you sound like you believe it. Believe that you are a carpenter; your van's broken down miles from nowhere in the dead of night. You're broke, dead tired and your wife is nine months pregnant.'

Apart from making me blush like mad and forget everything but the twinkle in Jacky's eyes, I suppose it was quite useful. That afternoon after school I went along to the woodwork room to get a quick sniff of sawdust. I did begin to feel like a carpenter, vaguely.

At six-thirty we went into room two to get the make-up on. Miss Gardeno did mine. I enjoyed her soft fingers touching my face as she whispered, 'Remember. Feel it and believe it. Believe every word you say. Feel that part, feel it. You're a poor carpenter, you've been driving all night. The engine packs up. The nearest town is ten miles away and your wife . . .'

She put a few black dots on my reddening face, to show I needed to shave I suppose and after finishing me off, she went to help Jacky attach the pink pillow under her robes. It was the worst hour of my life! I muttered a quick prayer under my breath, hoping that as it was that kind of play I would get a special hearing.

The waiting really got me down though; that and this nagging doubt in the back of my mind that, secretly, all the time Julian Armstrong-Mayes was plotting some kind of terrible, final revenge on me and Miss Gardeno.

I heard the cars pull up outside the school; the car doors slamming. People walking. Kids' shrill voices jeering across the dark car-park outside the windows of room two. It was five to seven.

Seven o'clock and Jacky and I were standing outside the doors to the drama hall. The icy stalagmite had grown into the back of my jaw. I felt sick, I wanted to run home and forget the whole thing. Why me? I couldn't act to save my life! Jacky started bumping her pillow against me whispering, 'You do know how to start off, do you?'

I heard Miss Gardeno introduce the play. A brief clapping, the lights go down, the door jerks open and Joe and Mary go stumbling down the darkened aisle towards the stage and the terrifying spotlight hanging there like some brilliant white spider's web.

'Oh Joe, my husband,' Jacky groans as I stagger across the stage like an ox to the slaughter. 'I can't go any further . . . my time is come near . . .'

My time seemed nearer. With a superhuman effort I took a deep breath and opened my mouth. 'W-wait . . . l-look! There is a light . . . A neon sign. Look, darling . . . it is a motel . . .'

But after that, acting became a lot easier suddenly, than I ever thought it could be. You couldn't see the audience anyway in the dark. You soon forget they're out there in the darkness waiting for you to make a mistake. With great confidence I knocked on the door. The motel owner appeared.

Being a kind, good man, I smile at him politely.

'Excuse me. We're in a terrible mess,' I told him. 'Our car's broken down. My wife . . . my wife's expecting any minute . . . and we wondered if you had any room in your motel?'

Jammy too was smiling warmly. He's forgiven us, I thought. Then, still smiling, he steps out of the curtains. Hold on, I think, this isn't right.

'Room?' He asks, rubbing his hands together. 'Room? My good fellow, of course there's room. In fact, there's plenty of room. Here, take your good woman and please, please go on in.'

It was like a bad dream. I felt Jacky jerk with shock and just stare helplessly at me. I heard this rustle in the audience and a distant crash from behind the curtains. So this was his revenge. Worse than that, only one person in the whole world could stop it.

Don't ask me where I got the idea from, but I stepped inside the curtain for a couple of seconds and then came bursting back out.

'What? You must be joking!' I shouted angrily. 'Me take my wife in there? Full up with drunks shouting and fighting all over the place, and gambling and women everywhere? I'd never take her into a dump like that. You want your head examined.'

Jammy's face changed. His eyes narrowed.

'I'd rather spend the night in the stables,' I told him firmly. He nodded and folded his arms.

'O.K. big mouth, you do that.' And turning on his heel he slouched back in.

So that was how our one and only third year Nativity play was saved from disaster. For the rest of the play I didn't have to say too much, but I felt like I was floating on air. The miners and professors did their bit very nicely and these psychedelic angels wound the whole thing up beautifully.

Afterwards the audience clapped and cheered, and Mrs Potter came diving backstage to congratulate the two of us — me and Jammy.

'I thought you two were marvellous. That row you had outside the inn. What an inspiration. Oh yes, the carpenter, poor but morally strong spurning the wealthy decadent capitalist. Superb!'

Neither of us knew what she was on about. Then she went off to see how Miss Gardeno had recovered from this mysterious fainting fit she'd had: the backstage crash I heard in the distance.

I then saw Jammy had cruised over to Jacky and was

chatting her up again. I went up and tapped him hard on the shoulder.

'I want a word with you,' I said, in my toughest voice.

'Oh yeah, hardnut?' he answered, pretending to square up to me.

'Here, stop it, you two!' Jacky rebuked us firmly, holding up this doll she'd been carrying round for half the night. 'Not in front of Him . . .'

'Eh? Oh, I see,' Jammy answered, blushing, and bowing low to the doll he walked quickly away, leaving us two together.

'You know your Miss Gardeno fainted,' Jacky said. 'That shows how much faith she had in you, doesn't it?'

'Well, it was a bit of a shock . . . what d'you mean, *My* Miss Gardeno?'

'I've seen the way you've been eyeing her up these past few weeks.'

'What? Her? Miss Gardeno?' I gasped in disbelief. 'You aren't jealous? But — she's only a teacher.'

'So?' Jacky flashed her tiger-grey eyes at me and I thought, well, one day I might understand quadratic equations; but women? Never!

I had to have a quick chew of gum to relax my tattered nerves after all that lot. Suddenly a voice barked behind me.

'What's this, lad? Chewing in class again?'

I spun round expecting to see Braddock, but it was Jammy, holding the pink pillow and three packets of bubbly on top.

'Christmas present,' he announced. 'From decadent capitalists the world over.'

Black, White and Grey

Why can't adults trust kids? It really is highly demoralising to be treated like an idiot or a criminal. There we all were sitting on the carpet of the drama hall in assembly waiting for Thornie, the headmaster, and wondering what he'd cuss us for today: the girls for wearing jewellery, the boys for wearing Doc Martens? Cementing our decrepit old school together with bubble gum? Or hiding the cracks with graffiti?

But no! Today was different. It was his turn to start off on the old favourite topic for Autumn Term. He gave his grey moustache a quick tug and started.

'Now then, third year, as you may already know you're going to have a new Maths teacher next term. Mr Gonzales. Let me just warn some of you — Mr Gonzales is a very gifted man: good university degree, two years experience in industry and glowing reports from his teacher training college — but that isn't what some of you will take into consideration . . .'

And off we were again. We all looked round, casting sour glances at each other. Stoney, our tutor, had given us the same chat twice last week; Badger, our head of year, mentioned it in Humanities and in assembly on Tuesday.

I mean, what difference did it make to us where this Gonzales character came from? A teacher was a teacher. Maths was Maths. The fact that he was coming all the way from Africa to teach us sounded more like a fairy story than anything else.

When the boss had finished his lecture and woke us up with the trigger phrase, 'Any questions?' Chico Marks put his hand up. The assembly rustled eagerly.

'Sir, is there any truth in the rumour that this Mr Gonzales bloke is really President Amin in disguise?' he asked, looking very pleased with himself.

We watched Thornie go beetroot and giggled to ourselves as quietly as possible. Thornie didn't say a word. He seemed to be saving his breath for something else. Instead he strode out of the hall, picking up Chico by the collar, en route, and the two of them disappeared with a cloud of dust and squeals of protest.

The same evening I just happened to say to Dad that our new Maths teacher was coming all the way from Uganda.

'Why should a bloke come all that way just to teach us? I mean, you'd think he'd have something better to do, surely?'

Dad was just about to open the pub doors, as it was gone five to, and he stopped in mid-stride.

'A Ugandan? Really?' he asked, eyes wide with surprise, then delight, as if I'd come top of the class. 'Good Heavens! What an enterprising Headmaster you've got. He really is. You know, schools like yours, and headmasters like him really are the answer to the nation's problems! Social equality and racial harmony. Splendid!'

He pushed himself a quick whisky from the optic and continued his sermon. 'It's just what you kids need. You never see any black people round here. That's why you're all so narrow-minded and prejudiced about race. Ah, but to be taught by a . . . a black person, just the job.'

There was an angry rattle on the door. It was after all four seconds past six. Dad ignored it. He had something much more important to do.

'Mind you though, you will treat him with the greatest respect, is that understood? No smirking, no silliness — or stupid jokes, right?'

Not again! I began to feel very angry. 'But Dad — he *is* a teacher!'

'What's that got to do with it?' he snapped. The door rattled again. 'If I hear the faintest rumour that you have in any way misbehaved, or ill-treated this person, who is after all a human being like anybody else, I shall publicly disown you.'

By the sound of the fierce rattling on the door his clients were just about ready to disown him. I nodded feebly and felt pretty mad by now. I mean, what did they all expect? 'He is after all a human being.' Well, what were we supposed to be then? I know the last Maths teacher we had left after one term because of a nervous breakdown but that wasn't our fault; everybody played her up.

Miss Brenton was just not right for our school. She should've taught somewhere safe and quiet like a convent or a children's hospital, or a grammar school!

I remember one bad lesson, well, they were all bad really, she stood in front of the class, stamped her foot and screamed, 'Why do you hate me?'

We all stopped whatever it was that we weren't supposed to be doing, and stared at her in astonishment. Then Murphy got down from the table and said, 'Nothing personal, Miss,' and we all carried on.

Until January the tenth. Lesson two was Maths with our new teacher; Thornie's latest sacrificial offering to us, all the way from Uganda. The class was really quiet for a change.

Then Chico whispered across the room. 'Hey, listen you lot — jungle drums — Amin's coming!'

These quick footsteps clicked down the corridor. He sounded quite keen actually. When he did walk through the doorway, I had a bit of a shock. I was expecting a real African, but this Gonzales character looked like an Indian. How confusing! Not for Chico, who'd obviously been rehearsing loads of jokes over the holidays.

'Cor, things look a bit black today, don't they, Murph?' he called across the quiet classroom in a very loud voice. Murphy laughed uneasily.

Mr Gonzales, Mr J.C. Gonzales B.Sc.R.C., was of average height, immaculately dressed in navy blue blazer, white shirt and old school tie. The two crossed hockey sticks on it looked like crossed swords. His hair was carefully permed and he was, as the girls all noticed immediately, very good-looking. Even worse than all that, he had the poshest voice I'd ever heard; even posher than my old man after two brandies.

He put down his books in a neat pile, then stepped briskly over to Chico.

'So, you must be Marks. Yes, you, the one with the big

voice and small brain,' he concluded crisply, leaning on the table. Chico, as yet unruffled, nodded. Mr G. stood up.

'Mr Thorne warned me about you. He said if I have any trouble from you I can kick your teeth in, O.K.?'

It wasn't just what he said but the way he said it. Chico went whiter than white and looked straight ahead. He knew when teachers meant it. Then Mr G. swung round and marched in front of the class to announce himself — a sort of 'Meet your new sheriff'.

'My name is Gonzales. You are 3L. I am going to teach you Maths. I don't care if we don't get on. I don't care if you hate me, as long as you don't leave my lessons as ignorant as you came in.'

As if on cue a ping-pong ball rattled on to the floor and pinged innocently towards him. Without looking he trapped it deftly under his foot.

'I know this class has a reputation for being disruptive and that you like playing teachers up. But that's all right, I am a firm believer in discipline and I spread the word wherever I go. I shall look forward to converting you heathens.'

The table tennis ball crunched like an egg-shell. Gonzales went to the table and started giving books out and the crushed ball stayed where it was all lesson.

The bell sounded like doomsday when it finally rang, it seemed so loud. After the quietest Maths lesson in living memory he left us to our devices. Then everybody erupted.

The lads all came out with these jokes they'd stored up, learnt off by heart but hadn't the heart to utter in class.

The girls all swooned and commented on the clarity of the instructions and good use of the blackboard. But, out in the yard, things looked pretty mutinous.

'Our dad says there are thousands of teachers out of work,' grunted Murphy after spitting at this crisp packet that was floating past. 'So why do we have to get lumbered with a blackie, eh? That's what I want to know?'

They all murmured, spat at all the other crisp packets floating round the yard and nodded. Chico giggled hysterically.

'Dunno about you suckers, but I thought I'd had it in there. I tell you, from now on I'm a good boy!' For once he looked as if he meant it.

Murphy shot him an evil glance and chewed a new stick of gum. Trencher's jaw dropped open eagerly. The third year village idiot was glad to join in on some dirty work.

'Here, I thought he'd be wearing a grass skirt, eh? And war paint!' The others blushed a bit and laughed feebly. 'Chico's only chicken cos he might get stewed in his pot for lunch!' Trencher continued.

'Oh yeah, thickhead?' Chico stood toe to toe with Trencher. 'Listen Trench, when some blackie calls me a heathen it's an insult, when he calls you a heathen it's a compliment!'

Everybody laughed at this, except Trencher who was still trying to work it out after lunch.

I must admit I didn't like this Gonzales much. My Maths might've been improving, but behaving that well was like being frozen in blocks of ice.

The strain was too great. Mind you, I didn't want anybody to think I had anything against him . . . especially as the girls seemed on his side from the word go. So I cleaned the board, collected books, opened the door for him and, along with Chico, was the model of co-operation. He thanked me politely, even giving me a quick flash of those pearly white teeth they all have.

'An Asian?' my father gasped, fascinated yet again, the next evening. 'Of course a Ugandan Asian, probably on the run from Amin. The Black Hitler, eh?' Mind you, what an asset to the nation! Some brilliant minds the Asians, you know. Had their civilisation while our ancestors were paddling coracles.

I looked at Trencher next morning writing 'Go Home etc. etc.' on the board and wondered if his dad had invented his coracle yet. When he'd finished mis-spelling the crucial word he heard footsteps and I rubbed it all off just as Mr G. strode through the cloud of white dust.

Trencher was in a particularly nasty mood that day. He's so thick he has special lessons instead of English, but he makes up for being stupid by being crooked. Any chance of theft, vandalism, arson and he's in like a shot. Today though, he couldn't do his Maths. The queue was too long for Gonzo to give him enough help so Trencher just strolled away as clueless as before and less patient.

'Wish we had a white teacher,' he moaned in a loud voice. The room fell quiet. 'Least I could understand what he was saying, these blackies can't even talk the language, our dad says . . .'

By now Gonzo had risen to the bait and stood up fuming.

'Shut up, Trencher!'

'Why the hell should I? Nothin' bloody else to do.' This was Trencher at his worst. Usually teachers ignored him if he was this bad. We all braced ourselves as Trencher continued. 'Bloody borin' lesson anyway. I hates Maths . . .'

The monologue was cut short by the Gonzales forehand smash across his left ear: the eighth this week. Trencher jerked and crouched in his chair for a second, then he leapt to his feet.

'That hurt, Gonzo!' he bellowed clutching his pink ear. Gonzo was aiming the backhand follow through. 'I'll get our dad on you — he hates niggers!'

'Get it right, you moron,' Gonzales hissed, 'I am an Asian not a negro. I hate to admit this, but we share the same Indo-European ancestry.'

'That's all right, our dad hates the Common Market as well! He'll get you for that!'

Mr Gonzales moved over to the door, flung it open and stretched out his hand. 'All right then, go and get your dad. And let's see if he's as stupid as you are.'

'He is, sir,' quipped Chico a second after Trencher had rushed out. None of us had expected it to get this far. Murphy sat back and pretended to be sympathetic.

'Shouldn't have done that, sir, they only live down the road, and his old man's out of work. He'll be up here quick as lightning.'

Mr Gonzales was not worried. 'Good, then the whole school can see what they're like.'

'But blimey, sir, we know what they're like,' moaned Chico, and we all laughed. Gonzales looked round, bewildered by the laughter, then realised who we were laughing at.

'You mean,' he said, 'you lot don't agree with him, or support him?'

'Course not sir, what d'you think we are?' Chico asked and got no answer. Instead Mr Gonzales looked suddenly relieved and relaxed. One moment he'd had his back to the wall surrounded by enemies, now, although he may have not been surrounded by friends, at least the real enemies had gone. The next question was: when were they coming back?

We had library lesson next. From the window you could see the school gates — and Mr Trencher practically running through them, sleeves rolled up, fag in his mouth, face beetroot with meanness. He was alone.

I asked to go to the toilet and crept down the stairs just as he stormed in.

'Where is he? Where's that blackie? He's hit my boy, he has. He belted my littl'un, he did, bruised 'im he has. I'll 'ave 'im, oh yes!'

I saw Thornie leap out of the corridor and practically smother him in his arms to shut him up.

'You leave me be. I want the bastard that belted my boy. I'll 'ave 'im. Oh yes!'

'Mr Trencher, the children are watching. You are showing yourself up. Now, please.'

This worked like a charm. Trencher stood there, mouth open, eyes swivelling round at all the imaginary kids' faces laughing at him. Then, like a lamb, he was led meekly away to the boss's office. Just before I nipped back I saw Mr Gonzales hurry along the corridor after them.

30

And that was it! Nothing very dramatic after all; certainly no punch-up. Half an hour later we were all at the library windows craning our necks to see Thornie with Gonzales and a very embarrassed Mr Trencher. And believe it or not, Gonzales actually shook Mr Trencher's hand. It couldn't have been the other way around.

I couldn't work out how Thornie had managed it. But Murphy who is reasonably friendly with the Trenchers found out very soon.

'Old Thornie told Gonzo to apologise to old man Trencher for hitting his son,' he told us in a quiet triumphant voice. 'Yeah, Thornie says, "Beltin' your son is your own privilege, Mr Trencher," or something like that . . .'

We all felt really disappointed and I don't know if the others noticed but after that Gonzales didn't lay a finger on any of us — well, not so often anyway. Still, in some ways he didn't need to, not now.

Another funny thing was just before half term, when we'd got to know each other and Trencher was in a different Maths group. I'd just collected the books, cleaned the board and opened the door. He beckoned me outside and said in a quiet, reasoning voice, 'When are you going to start treating me normally?'

I gaped at him. Me? The model pupil? I looked round to check he meant me.

'Do you carry the books for every teacher, and clean the board and open the door?'

I shook my head uncertainly.

'No? Then why do all this for me . . . ?'

'Well, sir, because I thought you . . . you need all the, er

. . . I . . . I felt very embarrassed suddenly and realised what he was getting at. All right then, clean your own flippin' blackboard, I thought to myself. And after that, Maths lessons weren't quite such a strain any more.

The Dispute

Someone was trying to stir things up. We had a mysterious bag-snatcher in 3L. You know, kids put a bag down in a classroom and the next thing it's gone! But this wasn't the usual silly joke, the one where you find your bag later on top of the lockers, or behind the door, or hanging out of the window. No, this outbreak was the work of some sort of school Mafia. That morning in class my bag was the intended victim. I had just bent down to get out my rough-book, when I saw the little white note in its place.

'If you ever want to see your bag again, leave 10p outside the library door at lunchtime.'

What should I do, I thought: give in, negotiate, or stay firm and refuse to co-operate? In the end I just stood up and said in a very loud voice; 'O.K., who's nicked my bag, then?' And before Boris could lumber over and investigate the source of this disturbance, the bag reappeared, suddenly and silently back by my chair. Someone had obviously been watching too much News.

One thing about Boris though, nobody liked him much, but there was always law and order when he was around; know what I mean? He was a big bald bloke with a thick curly beard and beady black eyes. He looked like a Russian so we all called him Boris, even though his real name was Stone.

There are three beards in our school actually: Boris, who's also our tutor, Badger, our Head of Year, who looks dead smart, like a French count, and of course Sandy, who looks like, well, nothing really. But what do you expect an art teacher to look like?

So anyway, at lunchtime, I was trying to work out the identity of the phantom bag-snatcher with Chico. He would have laid money on Trencher. But although Trencher mucked about a lot, he was far too thick to think up anything like that note. Then Chico suddenly appeared to have an idea.

'Hold on,' he said with a jerk forwards and looked up and down the corridor. 'Something's wrong, isn't it?'

The truck was half an hour late with the servery food, but that was nothing unusual. The kids were all milling about in the corridor, laughing, chatting, trying to push in, getting squeezed out . . .

'Where have all the teachers gone?' he asked. Flicking his fingers and knowing the answer already he continued; 'Because there's a strike on! Yeah, they're only all on strike, aren't they?'

I had heard vaguely about a strike, or something on telly. I wasn't interested though. I hate the news anyway. The only strike that would get me excited was one that kept teachers out of school altogether, and this one obviously didn't.

'There's a strike on. They aren't doing any dinner

34

duties, and that stuff my dad said, and he knows all about that sort of thing, 'cos he's a shop steward. I saw it on telly too. Loads of school kids getting kicked out at dinner time . . . hey, and yeah, these kids in Liverpool had a flippin' sit-in.'

Once that news travelled up and down the corridor, the queue sort of changed shape and became more like a series of small scrums. The sound changed too, more like Wembley stadium at Cup Final day.

But before anything else could happen, the queue reformed, quietened down and stood back against the wall, watching Chico telling us eagerly about sit-ins he'd seen other schools having on telly; and watching Boris loom up silently behind him, like a battleship creeping up on a dinghy. Chico turned round slowly in mid-sentence, then leapt back against the wall.

'Queue up properly and quietly for your lunch — or there'll be no lunch!' Boris boomed, fixing us against the wall with his beady black eyes.

'Why aren't you on strike with the others, then?' Chico dared ask, in disappointment more than anything, I suppose.

'Strike?' Boris whispered, taking one step forward. 'What strike?' he repeated, taking another step forward. 'There is no strike, Marks, merely . . . merely some members of staff, wishing to indulge in the national pastime of squabbling over money, are choosing to suspend certain non-academic activities: such as trough-patrol during lunch hour. But do not forget, Marks, that others, preferring their individual freedom perhaps, have chosen not to belong to any union and are therefore still

35

maintaining order and discipline. Do you understand, boy?'

'Well, I er . . .' Chico shrugged a bit. 'I get the general idea, sir.' And with that last word he became part of the orderly, quiet, hungry queue.

Art with Sandy was on the menu for the afternoon, so we could have a good chat and get the general political picture sorted out.

Sandy Sanderson, like Chico, was also dead keen on politics. He was always telling us to get organised and have unions for this and councils for that. Come to think of it, Sandy was the exact opposite of Boris.

Boris was strict and tough and scared everyone speechless. His lessons were real pin-droppers. Sandy was a skinny, scruffy character from somewhere up north, he had a gingery beard and thin gingery hair. He was soft as toothpaste and art lessons were consequently a real laugh.

He put this record on once, 'The Blue Danube'. You know; Da-da-da-dum! pom-pom! pom-pom! but with every 'pom' you slap on some paint on to your paper. So it's Da-da-da-DUM! splish-splash! red-blue! Da-da-da-DUM! green-purple! — all in time to the music and no splashing in between. Well, that, according to Sandy, was just one way to paint yourself a picture. He even had this special clever phrase for it: 'Musically stimulated colour creativity response'. And what a mess! The waves of the Blue Danube were splashing all round the art room that lesson, I can tell you — plus a few extra colours as well.

The biggest laugh, though, was the life-drawing episode. Funnily enough, Sandy started off by arguing with

Chico about human rights, of all things. Teachers really had no right to hit us, give us homework or even tell us off. Chico was agreeing so much that Sandy started telling him off for overdoing it.

So anyway instead of continuing the argument, Sandy sat on this high stool and started to take his clothes off. Right there in front of everybody, girls and all — right down to his striped shorts. What a nut-case, we all thought. Of course, he was acting as a life model, you see. Then we all got our clipboards and paper and started painting. Actually, I have to admit, Sandy himself was a fantastic painter. His landscapes and portraits of sixth-form girls were hanging all round the main entrance hall. Beats me what he wanted to waste his time teaching for!

As he sat there, he was telling us what to watch out for; light and shade, colours of the skin and things like that. And it was quite quiet and interesting in the end, I suppose. Then, before the bell, he comes round looking at our efforts: 'Very nice, not bad at all, good, beautiful — you flatter me, Rachel . . .' and so on. Until he gets to Chico's effort.

There was this long pause during which Sandy's face squashed into itself in horror. There was this match-stick man with balloon head, with two dots for eyes, and cruellest of all, these stringy red whiskers and twiggy red hair sticking out all over the place, like a thatched roof gone wrong.

'And what . . . is that?' he stutters, trying to control himself.

Chico glanced at it, then chirped back as cheekily as he could; 'Oh that? That's you, in' it? Blue Danube style!'

Now, there should have followed another lengthy discussion about human rights and individual liberty and all that, like there usually was when he tried to tell someone off. But not this time. Oh no, it was something much more comprehensible. Sandy grabs the board ruler, swings it round his head and chases his pupil all round the art room.

'Ere, wot about my individual liberty and freedom of expression?' Chico managed to scream out as he ducked and dodged the vicious swipes of the ruler.

'It's morons like you who deserve fascism!' Sandy screamed back. Luckily the bell went just then; the door flew open and Chico flew out, free until next art lesson, we suppose.

Strangely enough, though, Chico was really behaving himself well at the start of that next afternoon; no cheek, no silly questions, no mucking about of any kind; instead, mouse-like quiet, careful concentrated work and the phoniest look of admiration and respect that he could put on.

He was up to something all right and it wasn't just a routine creep session either. Then he got Sandy to start talking about this strike, or whatever it was. It turned out to be exactly as Boris had told us, not a real strike at all, but just banning certain activities such as 'trough patrol' as Boris so rudely put it. I mean after all, we eat with knife and fork. What more does he want?

'I reckon we ought to have a sit-in', Chico declared, 'like those kids in Liverpool.' Funny how he should suggest this straight after he finds out Sandy's a union man and all for the 'industrial action'.

'What is there to sit-in for, though?' Sandy asked in surprise. 'I mean, you still get lunches here, Chico. What could you protest about?'

'Eh? Oh yeah . . .' he realised and the glint in his eyes faded for a moment. Then he shrugged thoughtfully. 'Never mind I'll think of something.'

And he did too. Next lunch hour he was trying to organise all the third-years into having a sit-down demo in the school yard. In the end he only managed to round up ten of us and none of us really knew what it was all about.

'What exactly are we protesting about?' I asked him quietly, trying to get comfortable on the tarmac. 'I thought Sandy said we didn't have a case.'

'Ah, yeah, well, I told him this demo was to draw attention to our total lack of . . . er . . . representation at pupil level, see?'

The others all nodded dumbly. None of us had a clue, really.

Chico continued slyly, 'But what I have done is to make sure that Boris knows all about it as well . . .'

'Boris?' we all yelled in alarm and started to shift. But he stayed dead cool.

'Relax,' he soothed us, patting the air. 'I've got it all worked out. When I told Sandy, he said he'd come out and lend us his support, see? When I dropped a huge hint in front of Boris, he warned me that there'd be big trouble if I did, see? So all we got to do is sit here and wait till they all turn up. Sandy, and Boris . . . and the others of course.'

'Others?' we gasped, as he checked the time for some

reason. Then he squatted in the middle of our huddled circle and looked very business-like. He muttered something about phone calls, and the time, and then we all waited in silence.

And we went on waiting. No-one came out. No teachers, no others. In fact the rest of the school ignored us completely, which was the worst thing about it all. What's the point of having a demo if there's nobody looking on? I suppose they were too busy watching all the little punch-ups that had sprung up all round the field. We were all getting very bored and uncomfortable. The only reason we stayed was because none of us knew what Chico had really planned and he did make it sound something rather special. But it was Trencher who put our feelings into words for us.

'Here, I ain't 'alf getting a cold bum' he groaned, then looked up. 'At last! Looks like the others are coming, Chico.'

But it wasn't the others that Chico was expecting. We could tell that by the way the leader gave Chico a small kick in the back.

'What you load of poofs doing here, then?' It was Bob Jeffreys, the fifth form thug, grinning down at us, eager for fresh trouble.

'Hullo, Jeffo,' answered Chico smiling weakly. 'We're having a sit-down demo. Want to join us?'

'What me? No way. I'm a prefect aren't I?' He roared gleefully. Like hell he was 'What with no teachers about, might as well make sure there isn't any trouble. And you poofs are causing trouble, see? So I reckon I'd better sort you out. Now what do *you* reckon?'

'I reckon you're being unreasonable,' said Chico carefully. 'All we're doing is protesting over teachers' neglect. My dad says . . .'

'Yeah, I know about your dad. Our brother works up at Listers too and he reckons your Dad was a bloody trouble-maker. No wonder they bloody sacked him!'

While this was going on, three, then four more of Jeffo's thugs turned up to watch and wait. For a moment we all prayed silently that Boris would arrive before Sandy, and quickly. But still nobody came.

At last Chico got to his feet and began in a shaky voice.

'Er . . . brothers. Now that our discussion is at a conclusion, I recommend that we have a quick withdrawal and reconvene at a later date. Leg it!'

He side-stepped Jeffo and ran off towards the science block. Jeffo followed, bellowing joyfully. The rest of us were about to leg it as well, as the open field gaped a green invitation to us all. But then Chico came sprinting back round the corner of the science block and Jeffo came galumphing after him, till a loud voice stopped him in his cart-horse tracks.

'Robert Jeffreys! Stay right where you are!' and round the corner strode the three of them: Thornie and two policemen.

Thornie came over to us quickly and urgently as we were just getting on our starting blocks. But instead of asking us what happened, he guessed.

'You thought that the school was going to become one big playground for bully boys did you, Robert?' he rasped in Jeffo's ear.

'No,' Bob grunted sullenly back. 'They were causing

trouble. Having a sit-in, like. I th-thought I was doing you a favour, see?'

Thornie just gave Jeffo a long, tired look which meant, 'Don't ever do me any favours', then sent him off to his office, which was a relief to us. But it was our turn next.

'Having a sit-in, were you?' Thornie asked slowly. 'And I don't suppose any of you know who phoned the police?'

We shook our heads, not daring to look at Chico. Thornie looked a bit uneasy even though the police were right behind him. Then he added, 'I'll be seeing you lot again later, all right?'

Once we had raced off to the cycle sheds we all bombarded Chico with questions. But instead of answering them he beckoned us round to the front of the school. There, just outside the small front gate were two blokes: one tall and thin in denims, the other short, balding and fat in a blue rally jacket, carrying a large camera.

'Who the hell are they?' we asked, getting quite nervous.

'It's the newspaper blokes, in'it?' he informed us proudly. 'Why should those kids in Liverpool get all the glory? Now it's our turn, right?'

'What happened, kids?' the tall one asked, as we piled outside after Chico.

'You're too late,' Chico replied and turned and pointed to this Panda car parked outside the main entrance. The two policemen standing beside it were talking to Thornie.

'It's all over. And look, they've arrested the headmaster for assault!'

Instead of running off I watched the tall one whisper

'fantastic' and start to scribble like mad in his notebook. The other took a photo of us all.

'And what about the riot,' the tall one continued eagerly. 'How many were involved?'

'Hard to say,' Chico began, as we gaped at him. 'We had this sit-in, all eighty of us, then the teachers came along, thirty of them, and there was lots of chasing and fighting and stuff . . .'

As in a dream, we watched this idiot writing it all down. Well, seeing the Panda car and the two coppers standing either side of Thornie this bloke thought it was all genuine — or genuine enough. Then after his mate took a couple more pictures these two suckers thanked us and left quickly, without even bothering to take a picture of Thornie and his police escort.

Nothing happened that afternoon. We weren't summoned to Thornie's office or anything. But next morning . . .

He pounced at half past nine. Boris led a dawn raid on our Humanities lesson and carted us all off. Chico was the only one missing. We knew he was in school, but he hadn't been in tutor period.

Once we shuffled into the office we saw to our horror that they were all in there: Boris, Sandy, Badger, the headmaster and this policeman in a peaked cap with silver buttons on his shoulders. Thornie waved the Gazette at us. As he spoke, quivering with rage, the whole room seemed to shake slightly.

'Police called to quell riot? Scores of children rampage through school? Headmaster confronts police?'

He paused to get his breath back, and we hoped, his

temper. I could see my picture clearly on the front page.

'And do some of you find this amusing? Please notice that none of us are laughing. In fact I find this whole thing very serious indeed. I had a phone call from Mr Trencher this morning. He saw the front page photograph and naturally wanted to know what his son was up to. It seems Rex was led astray along with the rest of you. So together with the evidence of two teachers I am led to believe that the ring-leader was Duane Marks. So: I've suspended him from school for the rest of the week. He will spend that time writing apologies to the police, the editor of the Gazette and the school governors because the school's good reputation has been damaged almost irreparably. You see how amusing the whole thing really is? And you will also see why I expect nobody amongst you to put a foot wrong for the rest of the year?'

Thornie, now bright beetroot, turned to glance at the others behind him.

'There is enough sensational chaos going on in the world without totally irresponsible stirring-up by silly, immature minds. Do you get the message?'

We . . . er . . . got the general idea.

How to Beat the Rat Race

Imagine having to get up in front of our class, 3L, and give them a talk for five minutes on your hobby or interest. Worse than that, imagine doing it with two of the school governors in there listening as well. That was what I had to look forward to in Monday's English lesson. The class had been doing their talks all the previous week, but by Monday afternoon it was the turn of the Ms and Ps. I had the impression that somehow Mrs Potter wanted my talk to be extra good.

I saw this as my big chance to get a good report for Easter, so I put a lot of work into my talk on 'The Human Body'. Actually I was quite keen on becoming a doctor at that time. So I had all my stuff ready: pictures, notes, diagrams; everything mixed up and ready to fall on the floor at any moment. Just as I was about to stick this chart on the board, the door opened and in walks this tall, thin, pale-faced gent. I recognised him as Taggart, the local bank-manager — his son was a creepy big-head in the fourth year.

'Ah, come in,' Mrs Potter crooned, beaming, and

ushered him to the back of the class like he was at the cinema. She turned and nodded at me firmly, which I took to mean 'This had better be good'.

I'll say one thing: our class, one of the noisiest in the school, was dead quiet and really well-behaved. They all had this 'glad-it's-you-not me' look on their faces as I stood before them, clearing my throat.

'Ahem-hem ... er ... the human body is a ... f-fascinating and highly complicated machine ...'

Would you believe it, but I had to stop there because Chico has his hand up; a cheeky grin on his face.

'Please sir ... but what does "phuphuphascinating" mean?'

The class sniggered very quietly; then we all turned to check Mrs P.'s reaction. She merely focussed her beady eyes on him and glared until he had shrivelled up into the ground. Then putting on this big smile for the governor she told me to 'Get on with it, please'.

Mind you, I was so nervous, it was a miracle I managed to say anything at all. I soon got my own back on Chico, because when I came to the bit about lungs I slipped in a few comments about smoking and cancer. The whole class turned round to stare at him and he went red and sat on his hands quickly. So I mumbled and blundered on. The class, though quiet, were not really listening. I could see all these pencils busy doodling everywhere. But it was when I came to the part about blood that the trouble really started.

'You all know what blood is,' I mumbled, 'that thick red liquid stuff. If you cut yourself you lose it, and if you lose too much of it you've had it.'

Suddenly there was a funny groan from the back of the class. It was Mr Taggart swaying on the edge of the chair, eyelids flickering strongly.

''Ere!' shouted Chico as he stood up and watched the man slide off his chair on to the floor. 'This geezer's fainted! — He has — he's out cold!'

Well, of course that did it. The whole class leapt to its feet to get a decent view of one of the school governors flat on his back. There was this loud jabbering chat going on till Mrs Potter roared at us and dived to the back of the classroom.

In the end Murphy and Streeter, the biggest lads in the class, were appointed ambulance men and they had to carry the man out, down the corridor and into the office. We never laughed so much in all our school careers — till Mrs Potter came back and then we were for it! Once more the class was dead silent, but for a different reason.

It looked like the end of our brief visit from the governors so I carried on with my talk, trying not to laugh. Just before the end Thornie came in. He stopped at the door waiting for me to finish, gave me a funny nod and went over to Mrs Potter.

As he walked back down the room he scowled at us all saying; 'Any other class and I'd have said it was accidental, but with you lot . . .' He went out shaking his head, without finishing his sentence.

'If you give this same talk for CSE in two years' time,' Mrs Potter advised me sternly, 'please check that the examiner is not allergic to blood'.

After me it was Benny's turn. It was all right for him now that our guests had come and gone. Benny was a quiet, blond-haired kid with glasses and a hare-lip. He was hopeless at school and we all made fun of him.

In library last week Chico had said to him, ''Ere, Paddy, why don't you give a talk on "Intelligent Members of my Family"? That should be over in the wink of any eye.'

We all had a crude laugh at this. Then I said, 'Or if you want a subject with more substance, how about, "The Contents of my Pocket"? That should take at least five hours.'

His pockets were always crammed to bursting with hundreds of things. No wonder he had a funny walk. I must say he kept the subject of his talk a big mystery, probably to avoid more stick from the lads; and when he got to his feet that lesson he was holding this big box with holes in the side.

As we all sat back waiting to be entertained one way or the other, I wondered if Mrs Potter had fiddled it so my talk was on while the governors were in and not Benny's. But no sooner had Benny got to his feet than the door burst open and in rolls old Gilpin, the local cattle farmer, smiling all over his red face. I never knew that he was one of our governors.

'Hello, Mrs Potter,' he called cheerily. 'Sorry I'm late . . . was detained somewhere.' He laughed again and tapped the side of his crimson boozer's nose. As he strode to the back of the class he said to us, 'What d'you think, kids, some silly so-and-so was giving this talk on blood with old John Taggart in the room — oh ho — and old John he did pass clean out on to the floor he did. He can't even stand the mention of blood — oh ho — not him.'

He laughed fit to burst and the rest of the class joined in for the sake ot it, till Mrs Potter loomed over us like a thundercloud over our nearest horizon. I didn't think it was all that funny, actually. But at last Benny could begin.

'Got me two white rats here,' Benny said lifting the cardboard top. 'Pinky and Billy. That's Pinky on the left — hellova devil he is.'

Four neat pink hands gripped the cardboard edge. Then two pink quivering noses tested the air for danger. They sniffed chalk dust, old socks and woolly pullovers; thought all was safe and peered haughtily over the top at us, looking round from pupil to pupil. Then they gave each other a disgusted glance and dropped back inside again, with a quick rustle of straw.

'No such thing as a dumb animal,' he told us mysteriously. 'And a rat's a genius. You did never see such a sharp brain as what they've got.'

We could see a couple of white heads nodding eagerly at him.

'Rats and mice, I been keeping them for years now. I breed 'em too,' Benny continued and taking out Pinky, or Billy — they both looked the same to me — he let them run up one arm, round his neck and shoulders and down the other. The girls gave a delighted shriek of horror and Mrs Potter backed away into the furthest corner of the room.

Suddenly old Gilpin broke in. 'Here, sorry, kid, but you aren't by any chance a relation of old Paddy Mcmenemy the docker, are you?'

'Er . . . yeah,' grunted Benny rather annoyed at this

irrelevancy, 'he was our gramps's brother.' And he carried on with this sort of juggling act with the two white rats; letting them race up his arms and over his chest and down his back. Each time that it looked like one was going to drop on to the floor and escape, the girls gave a great squeal and Benny caught it easily in one hand. But that wasn't what impressed me. I couldn't help noticing the way he spoke; so clearly, using all these big words. In lessons he hardly said anything except 'forgotten it', and yet here he was entertaining — no, teaching, the whole class.

That is until Old Gilpin got to his feet and stolled up to the front.

'No, no, kid, don't stop, don't mind me, this is most interesting. But don't, er, forget to tell 'em about Paddy Mcmenemy and his mice, eh?'

Benny was about to continue; then he screwed up his face and frowned doubtfully at Gilpin, who was standing by the door beaming all over his face, dying to tell us about Paddy's mice.

'You listen to this, kids,' Gilpin began eagerly. 'Old Paddy was a docker down in Sharpness and you'll never believe this, but he used to race mice. Honest. He had all these mice running round his house, so he goes and catches about half a dozen and holds race meetings. 'Tis true, mind. Many's the Saturday we used to go up Paddy's place with a quart of home-made scrumpy. Paint numbers of the backs of these mice, put 'em in this long wooden box, which had sort of lanes in it, place our bets and they're off! Oh ho, you did never see anything like it. All these men bent over the box on the floor, faces lit by

50

lamplight and the flare of a match, and the little mice all scampering like the clappers, oh ho. I had this one mouse, he won me thirty bob in one night — lot of money in those days, mind you. Yes ... well ... ahem ... er ... you carry on, lad. You ... er, tell 'em about your rats, then.'

He coughed awkwardly and we glanced at Mrs Potter who had this puzzled frown on her face. Then she smiled weakly at Gilpin, who smiled weakly at her; and Benny, frowning at everybody, resumed.

'If you want to keep pets of any kind you got to look after 'em real good. They ain't toys you just stick in a cupboard when you're bored with 'em and that. They're living creatures who can suffer pain or hardship just like people.'

We all nodded wisely at Professor Mcmenemy as he continued, or tried to continue, his lecture.

''Ere, sorry kid — but I remembered something else about Paddy. Why don't you tell 'em about Betty Monkton, eh?'

I'd have thought it was pretty obvious why Benny didn't tell us about it.

'Old Paddy — this'll make you laugh — he was a right old Casanova in his youth, and anyway he fancied this country girl called Betty Monkton. Betty, well, she came from a small village who didn't take kindly to strangers. Oh no! And what's more, she had five brothers and a dad who was more like a bull than the bull himself. So Paddy, who wasn't the brightest of mortals, goes up to old man Monkton and asks for his daughter's hand. Old man Monkton gives him an evil smile and says, "Of course, son, but you got to do one or two things first; an initiating like". Oh ho, they got 'old of him, tipped him upside down, shook the money out of his pockets, ripped the trousers off him and old man Monkton rode him bare back all the way up Tock Hill and down the other side. Oh ho, it may have been a cloudy night down in the Vale, but t'was full moon up on Tock Hill, eh? And . . . er ahem . . . anyway . . . sorry, lad, you er . . . you carry on . . .'

I'm not sure which is harder to describe, the look on Benny's face, or the look on Mrs Potter's. But, thank goodness, he let him finish his talk, twelve minutes of it, without further interruption. After the applause had pattered away, Gilpin stepped forward and put his hand on Benny's shoulder.

'Well, I reckon that was a smashing little talk, kids, really wonderful and it just shows you.' He leaned on the table and brought Benny round beside him, so that they both stood in front of the box. 'Some things you got to work for in life, and some things you're born with. And I can see that Benny here's got a real way with animals. A gift. Something you couldn't get from a million books. It comes from a natural born understanding of living creatures. Now his great-uncle may have been a fool, but our Benny isn't, oh no, he's got something he could really put to good use when he leaves school. So remember, kids, if you got a gift of any kind, don't ever . . .'

He had turned round at this point and was peering into the cardboard box. Then he looked up frowning.

'Dear me, lad, those little fellows aren't here. They've gone!'

There was a loud gasp of 'Oh no' from Mrs Potter who

leapt on to the nearest chair. A scream from all the girls, who took off in a similar manner, and then the whole class turned into an arena of man and boys struggling, diving, tumbling after two fleeing white rats.

Just as we nearly grabbed Pinky, or Billy, the door opened and Thornie, of all people, strolled in. The words froze in his mouth as he saw the chaos.

'Close that door, Bob!' bellowed Gilpin. But Thornie just looked down at the two white rats that shot between his flat feet and gaped at the onslaught of man and boys that thundered towards him.

Mrs Potter and Thornie managed to reduce the thirteen man posse to three: Gilpin, Benny and I.

'Come on, lads, tally ho!' roared Gilpin as we raced down the corridor into the entrance hall after our quarry. There was no sign of them. The rats had vanished. A series of screams from the office told us of their whereabouts and then two furry streaks of lightning shot across the tiled floor and disappeared through the half-open glass doors behind us.

'What goes on in there, lads?' Gilpin asked us before daring to go in. There were curtains hung all round the glass doors of the drama hall so no-one could see what the actors were getting up to. Just as well, sometimes.

'Drama hall, eh?' he echoed once we'd told him. He listened carefully to the screams and shouts coming from behind the curtain. 'Sounds like they certainly got drama in there today. Right, come on, lads! Tally ho!'

We all rushed into the hall together, like the three musketeers. Miss Silverberg, the drama teacher, came storming over. She was good-looking, too, with long dark hair and black eyes. She was just going to throttle Benny and me when Thornie entered, breathlessly, behind us. Miss Silverberg put her hands on her hips and waited for his explanation. I was quite keen to hear what he was going to say as well.

'Its . . . it's Mr Gilpin, one of the governors,' he told her, as they both stood watching the short plump figure crouching and leaping after two white shapes while the kids went epileptic everywhere else.

'I· wasn't informed beforehand,' she told him. He winced at something and sagged.

'He's chasing these white rats,' Thornie continued to explain, as the hubbub grew louder and other boys joined in the hunt.

'Chasing white rats?' she replied. 'Oh well, of course, that makes all the difference, doesn't it?'

There was an almighty cheer and Gilpin and Benny both emerged, grinning and triumphant, carrying two white rats, who also seemed to be grinning and triumphant. Miss Silverberg looked at her watch.

'Well, as there are still ten minutes of my lesson left, you might as well let them go again . . .'

Not surprisingly, when it had all quietened down Benny and I ended up in the boss's office. All the governors were there. In fact, Thornie was the only one who wasn't smiling.

'Any other class,' he growled. 'Any other pupils and I'd have accepted that it was an accident.'

'Oh, come on now, Bob,' Gilpin interrupted cheerily. 'You've got two very bright lads there. This kid gave a smashing talk on rats and John Taggart says the other boy was most intelligent in his knowledge of anatomy and that. Go on, give 'em a break, eh? After all, accidents do happen, don't they, even when the governors pop in?'

He nudged the headmaster and gave us both a heavy wink. Benny took the lid off his box and waited. The two pink-eared, white-headed judges peered over at the gathering and, nodding straight at Gilpin, pronounced us 'Not guilty'.

Winners and Losers

What is it about summer that makes me go all glowing and poetic? Is it the cuckoos shouting at each other across the wood at the bottom of the sports field, I ask myself? Or the return of the twittering house martins to their nests under the guttering? Is it the way you can walk out of the house and hear people talking and laughing everywhere, inside and outside, as if all the doors of the world are wide open?

Or could it be the way school becomes freer and more open? I mean, the way you can persuade suckers like Mr Sutherland to let you go out on the field and have a humanities lesson; like this:

'Eh, sir, please sir, let us go out on the field, go on, plee-eez.'

He blinks at us, overwhelemed with so much sudden popularity and politeness.

'Well, I don't know. I suppose you could if you . . .' He then disappears under a cheering, squealing, struggling scrum as the whole of 3L tries to squeeze itself through the door at once. After that it's all shepherd and sheep.

'Promise to behave . . . sensibly.'

Sports day was only a month away and I was just about to start my lazy jog-up for the long jump. Athletics bored me. I was a cricketer. The lads were watching me and waiting for a laugh. Then with a funny weak groan they all turned and started watching something else. I paused and followed their gaze. What a bunch of love-sick idiots! It was only Dawn Devonshire and she was for the high jump. I tried to ignore her as she stroked her tanned thighs, all tensed and ready to spring up like a gazelle. She raised her head in determination, took deep, deep breaths that had us all swooning in disbelief. No, I cursed myself. It's only Dawn.

But oh yes, it was the games lesson that made summer so good. I had to weaken, like the spineless male that I was and just watch as she soared up high over the bar, missing it by inches as all our hearts missed a beat.

'Huh!' I grunted loudly. 'So what. Dawn Devonshire? Huh! She thinks she's it. Just 'cos she's in three different events. But I bet anybody could beat her in the eight hundred metres. Anybody — even Brownie!'

The elephant grass at the side of the field parted and Chico, having woken from his siesta, suddenly leapt out at me with an eager twinkle in his eyes.

'How much?' he asked.

I shrugged uneasily. When I muttered 10p all the lads laughed. So I pretended to be joking and announced '50p' in a loud, confident voice. Chico gave me ten to one against. It's funny, really, but no one even thought of betting till he came along. He arrived one day out of the blue, all the way from London. Someone said his parents split up or something. Anyway, he goes bookmaking with his new dad at the local point-to-point. And now we bet on anything!

They all thought I was mad, though. I mean Brownie, Belinda Brown, was ugly to look at and stupid to talk to. But I reckoned she was a natural athlete. She'd better be. 50p was a lot of money as far as I was concerned. When she only just qualified in the heats it looked like I was giving my money away to Chico. She was mad as a March hare, too, which didn't exactly inspire people's confidence in her. Only I realised that beneath that fat blank face and curly ginger hair was a lot of potential. I knew just how strong she was — she hit me once and that was enough.

The lads all gaped at me and shook their heads once I'd taken up the challenge and accepted the bet. To be honest I was in a really bad mood that morning. You see, I used to think Dawn was pretty fantastic, too. She really was my kind of girl. When describing her to other people, you needed a dictionary to do her justice. The night before I'd taken her home from youth club. I'd danced with her from eight to ten, including the smooches, and I could see all the lads going green-eyed and trying not to look. She was the best looking girl in the whole school; apart from Miss Gomez, the Spanish teacher, and she was out of bounds. So, at five past ten that evening we pause at the top of the steps, she looks me in the eye and says, 'You *are* walking me home, aren't you?'

I nodded so hard my head nearly dropped off. Never mind how far away she lived.

Mind you, it was miles. All down dark country roads

and winding lanes, with this wind ruining my hair-do and cooling my ardour.

The other thing was she walked so flipping fast. I had to jog to keep up with her. I've only got little legs.

I kept saying, 'Let's go and see how many cows there are in that field,' and things like that, but she just kept straight on.

Finally we reached the front door of the farmhouse. I was nearly on my knees. She stood there smiling at me, all tall and slim and lovely, and three times as fit as I was.

'Thank you. I enjoyed that!' she whispered. 'Now then, open your mouth and close your eyes and you shall have a pleasant surprise . . .'

At last. I stood there, eyes shut tight, mouth open wide, wondering what she was going to do first, and how she was going to kiss me and what I was going to tell the lads next day, and after ten seconds I started to squint and peep through flickering eyelashes.

I opened my eyes just in time to see the door slam in my face. My mouth stayed open for a few seconds, then my teeth ground fiercely together till my jaw bone nearly cracked.

That was the end of my first and last night with our Miss World; an exhausting walk home, alone in the pitch dark, with only the gnats for company. She was no longer my kind of girl. In fact, I hated her after that. Not only did I want her to lose the big race, but I wanted to see her beaten by Brownie, who was the complete opposite — in everything.

My theory was that all Brownie needed was confidence and reinforced concentration, like they say on the telly.

Two weeks before sports day and I began to train her. I sat with her at lunch to make sure she ate well and then we'd go on the field for a training session: french cricket.

I'd hit the ball right down the end of the field, and she'd chase after it frantically. All the time I'd try and boost her morale, as they say. Naturally some of the lads would tease me and make out that I was dating her. But I just stayed coolly professional about it and said, 'This is purely a business relationship.' Well after all, 50p was 50p — and if I won!

They'd simply kill themselves laughing and shake their heads. They still thought I was mad. You see, the other thing about Brownie was she'd never come to school five days a week, at least not very often. Stoney would look at us over his register and ask 'Belinda here today?' as if he didn't know that we knew that he knew that she was skiving again.

But our training schedule was going very well. I even gave her my share of soya-bean mincemeat so that she could have extra protein. As for the french cricket — when we started I could score forty-nine with each smack of the ball, but now I ony managed twenty. She would need that speed for her sprint finish, I decided.

When sports day came at last, it was one of those cloudy, windy days that could rain any minute, but somehow never seemed to. I reckon sports days are marvellous occasions for the whole school, really, when you come to think of it. Such a colourful and relaxed atmosphere. Everybody's happy, enjoying an official skive.

The teachers love it best of all, I swear they do. They put their little sun hats and summer suits on and wander around with tape measures and clip boards, looking quite important for a change. Mrs Potter does her DJ act into the microphone speaking as slowly as an action replay.

'AND HEAH ARE THEE REE-ZULTS OF THE FIR-STA YEAR GIRLSA HUNDRED MEETAHS . . .'

The rest of them sit at this long table working out the scores like they were doing the pools.

But would you believe it, the day of the big race and Brownie's out of school again! Now I didn't believe she was ill for one moment and just hoped, foolishly, that she'd turn up later on in the day, as a special favour for me, or something. But by ten minutes to three there was only one thing for it. When nobody was looking I began to walk backwards up the field. Then I turned and ran like mad for the main building, yanked Gary Streeter's ten-speed bike from its stand and pedalled like mad out of the main gate and down to Brownie's house.

Everybody knew where the Browns lived. It was only half a mile from school, but it was the worst house in the terrace. There were always loads of kids swarming all over the place, like little pink maggots. They used to sit in the windows, on the grass, on the wall; they seemed to be everywhere.

When I screeched to a halt outside their gate the house was fairly quiet. There were two really scruffy kids out in the front. One had chocolate all over his face and was pushing a yellow plastic tractor over his sister. She was screaming the place down, but no one came out or anything. So I walked up to the front door and rang the bell, even though the door was wide open. The house was sort of naked with the door open like that. You could see right through to the kitchen.

'Yeah, what's want, then?' said this big ginger girl, who was one of Brownie's elder sisters. I told her.

'Lin? She's out the back. What you want her for, then?'

It took nearly ten minutes to come up with the right answers, and at last I was shown into the back garden.

There was a pile of tyres on the grass and next to them was Brownie in these horrible turquoise slippers and tatty old apron, hanging out the washing. She looked quite different; so much older.

'Hey,' I shouted angrily. 'What the hell are you doing the washing down here for? Your eight hundred metres is on in half an hour!'

'Can't 'elp that, my son,' she said, her mouth full of red plastic clothes pegs, making her look like a vampire. 'Our mum's gone away again. I gotta do all the washing now. Our dad'll kill me if he comes home and finds I haven't done it yet.'

Knowing her dad, he'd kill me too if he staggered home from the pub and found me there, trying to persuade his daughter not to neglect her precious education. I shivered with panic and could see myself clocking up shame, humiliation and minus 50p, all in one go. Besides, seeing her do the washing like that made sports day seem like some foreign custom.

I must go to choir practice again. It'll give me a chance to thank God for that short, sharp, thundery shower he sent me. I'd just got back through the school gates when the cloudburst started. It lasted till half past three. Brad-dock, the sports master, was furious. He tried to ignore it and stood in the rain checking his stopwatch, to see if it was waterproof, I suppose. Then he realised that he was the only human being left on the field. Everyone was inside — watching him get wet.

But it takes more than a quick burst of the monsoons to dampen his enthusiasm. If it rained on Wednesday he would have the rest of the sports day on Thursday and finish it all off properly.

It was still windy and grey on Thursday but there wasn't a drop all afternoon. Brownie was there too, miracle of miracles. I'd checked and double-checked just before lunch.

We had science after break and the labs are just by her room. She doesn't always have the same lessons as us. She goes off to this big room on the second floor and some-times she spends all day there.

I nipped in to check; she was sitting all on her own at this table. The teacher was on the other side, reading to two small boys. I went to Brownie and reminded her about the race.

'All right, I know,' she snapped back. 'What do you think I am? That's the third time.'

It was the fifth actually. I looked over her shoulder at the book she was reading. She saw me staring and covered it up quickly, but not before I could see all the large spaced-out print and pretty pictures. I don't know why she was so shy about it all of a sudden. We all knew she wasn't very good at reading and things like that, but I couldn't see her dad installing a library for Christmas, so why worry about it. As long as she was good at doing the washing and running the eight hundred metres that was enough.

The teacher looked up at this point, saw me and told me to get out. So I did. He only tells you once and then he does something about it. Besides I'd been long enough for the excuse I'd used, so I was due back in science.

In the afternoon, sports day was eagerly resumed. Our one-way family favourite DJ Inky Potter started us off with a joke.

'AND WELCOME BACKA TO SPORTSA DAY PARTA TWO.'

Everybody laughed, being in a good mood. After all, one and a half skives out of two afternoons was a real bonus.

We all sat on the wrong side of the rope, or sprawled out on our stomachs like a seal colony. Already Dawn was striding about the field like some goddess because she'd won the high jump.

'THE THIRDA YEAH GIRLSA EIGHT HUNDRED MEETAHS FINAL.'

I led Brownie across the field like a horse through the paddock, even getting a wolf-whistle from one of the lads. I crossed my fingers so hard they bent like rubber. The starter's pistol cracked like a cap-gun and they were off.

Brownie really took off like a rocket; much too fast for a race of that length. She led the whole field immediately. Then she started leaving them way behind.

'Slow down,' I yelled. She had forgotten every single piece of advice I'd given her. 'Slow down! Pace yourself.'

Dawn was really struggling — eclipsed, if you like, for the time being by this runaway mule who was sure to pack up and collapse from exhaustion any minute. But as they went round the lower bend of the field into the head-wind, Brownie actually accelerated, lengthening her stride and practically sprinting along. She was murdering them.

Then, as she came to the end of the first lap, she began to slow down. At last, I thought. But not this slow. What the hell's she doing? Slowing right down, arms waving stupidly in the air and all smiles? She's slowing down completely!

'I won!' she bellowed at everybody, then seeing me she jogged over. 'I won!'

I nearly fainted. 'No, no, no!' I screamed. 'You silly cow. You've got to run two laps! Remember? Twice round the field. Two times! Now go on, keep on going 'till they string up the yellow tape. Go on!'

The other girls, led by the reddening Dawn trotted past us and some of them grinned. Miss Piggot, the girls sports teacher, started to come over.

'Eh? What, all that again?' Brownie moaned, and put her hands on her hips. 'No chance, my son! Besides, I'm retired.'

'Please, please, please,' I begged, foaming at the mouth as the other girls began to become dots on the horizon. 'Just once more. Just once. Please. Just — just for me.'

'Gimme a kiss, then,' she piped craftily and went all girlish and pinky. What the hell, I thought. Anything better than the crushing failure that was staring me in the face. I hardly remembered smacking the faintest of kisses on that fat pink cheek — carefully missing the mouth, of course.

Then I grinned weakly at Miss Piggot, who was waiting for something as well.

'A bit of a pep talk, Miss Piggot,' I explained. She gave me a hard look with her javelin-thrower's eyes and then spoke. 'Get off the track!'

And as I turned I saw that Brownie was also just a dot on the horizon. I never knew I was such a good judge of horseflesh. She'd caught them up already. Very slowly, as if the rest of them were running backwards, she began to overtake them, one by one. As the headwind slowed the third and fourth runners down, Brownie floated past them like the super-athlete she really was. And suddenly the whole school was behind her, yelling her name, willing her to go faster.

Now only Dawn's ahead of her. And they're coming down the final straight. One furlong to go. And it's Dawn holding out for the final tape, with Brownie challenging strongly on the outside. Now it's Dawn and Brownie neck and neck. Dawn pulls away with the thunder of Brownie's hooves close behind her. They're dead level again. Everybody's going wild. Miss Piggot is pogoing like mad. Teachers and pupils screaming themselves hoarse.

'Come on, Brownie! Come on, Brownie!'

The noise winds itself up to a squealing crescendo before the tumultuous cheer, as it's — Brownie, yes beautiful Brownie breaking the tape first. Brownie the winner by half a neck!

'There should be a steward's enquiry,' grunted Chico as I rushed up to him with outstretched hand. Five lovely quid. Mine all mine.

'Brownie must be on dope to run like that,' he added, making no movement towards his pocket. Instead his eyes lit up as he stared over my shoulder.

'Oh er, by the way loverboy, here comes your sweet-heart. Going to give you your kiss back I shouldn't wonder.'

I swung round just in time to see her gallumphing towards me, pink arms outstretched, bellowing blissful-ly, 'I won again! I won. Gimme a kiss.'

Super-athlete she may be, my kind of girl she never was. Now it was my turn to run. The final straight — straight home. Five furlongs. But you'd never believe it — I really did sprint. As I hared away up the field, cheered on sarcastically by the lads, her pounding hoofbeats and heavy breathing got fainter not louder. I should have gone in for a race or two myself and put some money on me.

It wasn't the end of my troubles, though. Miss Piggot had overheard my jubilant words of money to Chico. Miss Piggot did not approve of any kind of vice! Nor did Thornie, because next day Chico and I were on the carpet in his office. We both glanced at each other, took a deep breath, and braced ourselves for another marathon speech. And off he went.

'One addiction I hate even more than smoking,' he growled, 'or alcohol,' he added fiercely, 'is gambling. Tobacco may rot a man's lungs, but gambling will rot his soul. Now I haven't got any proof of a gambling racket going on under my nose, but please, gentlemen, don't let me catch either of you even thinking of making a book in my school. Understand?'

I nodded and so did Chico. I bet he didn't even know what an addiction was. Still he used Thornie's warning as his excuse not to fork out! And when that started to lose its effect, he thought up something even worse. The minute I approached him with outstretched hand all he had to say was; 'Look out, loverboy, here's Brownie!'

Words like a starter's gun. I was off and away, a dot on the horizon, like the mad March hare I really must have been.

Merry England

It had to happen sooner or later, I suppose. We all rolled wearily into third year assembly that Tuesday morning ready for old Badger to read us another poem which didn't rhyme, or play us a folk song record by a bloke who couldn't sing, or look at some slides of stark naked pygmies. But no, today was quite different: plans for the Summer Fair.

'Now I think we should do something really special,' he told us firmly but eagerly. 'There's enough talent in this year group to put on something quite spectacular.'

Chico Marks gave me a soft nudge and whispered, 'Wait for it. Another dose of poncing about in fancy dress coming up.'

And he guessed dead right too. The fancy dress Badger had in mind consisted of the majestic robes of the kings and queens of England.

'In other words a pageant,' he continued, trying to cut in short as he saw our faces getting longer and longer. 'What with all the Royal Jubilees and Weddings we've been having recently, I think we should do a pageant on

69

kings and queens of Merry England. That'll cheer your parents up and remind them that we weren't just a nation of shopkeepers. At least, not all the time.'

Old Badger — curly dark hair, steel-rimmed glasses and moustache — was quite a smart bloke, really, in his navy blue blazer. He was often reminding us of the glories of the lost British Empire and things like that, as if somehow it was our fault we'd lost it.

Much to everybody's surprise Chico offered his services almost immediately after Badger had finished speaking. But Badger thought that Chico's impression of Prince Charles would be 'in bad taste under the circumstances', as he put it.

'Such a pity,' sighed Prince Charles. 'I could've told them abyte Mum telling Ded orf for leaving his pyolo sticks all abyte the hyse.'

Even so we soon had quite enough to get on with. We didn't do all the kings and queens of course. We had Arthur and Alfred, then all the rest from the Conqueror onwards right up as far as Edward the Seventh, with a few boring short-lived ones left out.

We were all grouped off and one in each group would come forward, say his or her bit and introduce the others. I was King Alfred. Yes, that's right, messing up some old lady's rock cakes as usual. Chico was Richard the Third, with black gloves and a cushion stuffed down the back of his tank-top.

It was funny, really, just who did get a part as king, or queen; not just the goody-goodies, but all sorts. Chico, for instance, despite his reluctance in that assembly was quite chuffed with his Richard the Third. He had a line from Shakespeare or something and he used to shout it out all over the place.

'Well I've seen the film, haven't I? That Laurence Oliver bloke, nice one!'

And from then on in the summer term, whenever he played cricket and on every rare occasion that he managed to score a run, he was off, scampering down the pitch shouting, 'An 'orse, an 'orse, my kingdom for an 'orse.'

The really great sensation, though, was the way old Badger managed to rope Maria Kelly into his pageant. Now Killer Maria was one of those really tough girls who scared everybody. Tall and thin, with cropped boyish, auburn hair, she could beat up any boy in our class with one hand freshly nail-varnished. Her dad was a docker at Sharpness — at least he was the last time she saw him.

At first even Badger had a rough ride, considering all the girls fancied him. When he asked in Humanities that afternoon if she could be Elizabeth the First, of all people, she just snapped back, 'You must be joking,' and folding her arms looked out of the window. 'I'm not making a fool out of myself in front of the whole school. No way.'

Badger kept his cool, sighed sadly and shrugged. 'It's a pity. She could almost be your ancestor. You two look so alike.'

There was no getting away from it, he was dead crafty. He pretended to leave it at that, but by a strange coincidence, suddenly there's this picture of Elizabeth the First lying about on a table just by the book case, whose glass doors acted as a mirror.

Now Maria gets up to borrow a pencil, ruler or rubber,

like she always does, and she passes this picture, stops dead, stares at it, gazes into the glass, steps back, turns her head to one side, then the other. Well, she's poring over this picture for about ten minutes and old Badger hasn't said a word to her. He just watches out of the corner of his eye. When she finally sits down again, her white hard face is all soft and pinky. He was right though; I got up and had a quick look myself — the old Queen was just like her.

At the end of the lesson Maria stayed behind for a few minutes and we all knew why.

Things were going quite well, I suppose, until that full rehearsal two weeks away from the real thing. All thirty of us were gathered together in the drama hall waiting for Badger. Chico, not happy at losing his dinner break, had it in for the Georges for some reason, and the cushion that was supposed to be down his back sailed among their royal presences.

'Here, 'ow d'you like this down your throat, you 'unch-back?' George the Second snarled.

'Oh yeah?' Richard sneered, staying out of reach. 'Well, at least I'm a real English king, not like you bunch of Germans!'

At first the Georges treated this insult with contempt until he carried on, 'It's true. You ask Badger, I looked you lot up. All of you Georges are German!'

They didn't like that one bit, but worse was to follow. Elizabeth shifted away from the wall she was leaning against to restore some peace and order, but he even dared turn on her.

'Don't you tell me to shut up, Taffy. That's right. You

aren't English either!'

That started it. According to Chico half the kings and queens of England were Welsh, Scots, French or German. By the time Badger arrived the pageant had turned into a royal punch-up, with the Georges chasing the Stuarts round the drama hall and the Tudors trying to brush Richard the Third under the carpet.

'This is a pageant of the kings and queens of Britain,' Badger roared at us having quelled the civil war. Then he crossed something out on his clipboard.

'That's how the British have always stayed powerful, by bringing in good foreign stock when their own monarchs were getting too weak to cope.'

We glanced at each other curiously. He sounded like he was talking about horses.

'That's the touble with the country kids,' he added quietly. 'Too much inbreeding.'

Actually the full rehearsal didn't go too badly in the end. I suppose once half of them found out they were foreign, there was less showing-off than usual.

A week later Mrs Potter started sorting out the costumes — hired, borrowed, heaved out of attics or just home-made, like my Anglo-Saxon gear. If you ask me King Alfred looked more like a hippy motor-cyclist in rugby socks with his shirt hanging out. Some of the others did look pretty good, I must admit. Elizabeth was really quite glorious in her long sequinned dress and high white collar that came up behind her like a shoe horn. She really began to look the part. Floating round the drama hall neither looking at, nor speaking to the rest of us, just gliding in majestic silence.

'Here,' whispered Richard the Lionheart, in awe of her, 'you don't think she is, do you? You know . . . a real ancestor of Queen Elizabeth?'

'Shouldn't think so,' I grunted jealously. 'We'd have heard the real one turning in her grave if she was.'

Anyway, I suppose it made a change from the usual summer fête we had to put up with every July. Besides no other year group was doing anything spectacular. It seemed only the third year was patriotic.

As I strolled round the stalls at one o'clock that warm windy Saturday afternoon I noticed all the old favourites were dug in expectantly. Mrs Bird's cake stall (and the headmaster's collie being politely warned off); old Bagsnatcher and his dartboards that needed a crossbow to reach them; and Pinhead with his bowls of water and coins at the bottom that always stayed uncovered. At least they'd decorated the yard with flags, coloured paper and canvas awning. Already the first parents were wandering ever-so-slowly across the field led by eager little kids who were trying to cure their boredom and bewilderment.

But apart from that there was one extra bonus. This Russian ship had docked at Sharpness a couple of days ago and according to Badger, old Thornie had threatened to invite their skipper along to the Summer Fair.

'D'you think he'll open it for us?' asked one of the smaller girls, as we gathered in the hall at two o'clock.

Badger sniffed doubtfully. 'Shouldn't think the Kremlin would like it,' he answered. 'Considering what we're celebrating, he'd get six months in Siberia if he did. I'd be surprised if he turned up at all.'

Then he took a deep breath and gave us a quick briefing. After this came the sweaty wrestling match to get into our tightly-buttoned helmetted costumes; hairy wigs that got into your eyes and mouth, and ancient footware that turned the Royal heritage into a long line of funny walks.

I peered out of the corridor window as we waited for some unexpected delay, then at last I saw Mr Nichols come leaping from his sports car, trumpet in hand. Once in the middle of the small orchestra he waved his trumpet at someone and they began to play 'Land of Hope and Glory' — faster than usual too.

We lined up in order as the wind carried snatches of the discordant tunes to and fro. I gazed over Arthur's shoulder and William the Conqueror breathed down my neck. I felt the whole line shoving and heaving forwards impatiently, but it wasn't our cue yet. At the first bar of 'Rule Britannia' I gave Arthur a shove and we stepped out, just as Mrs Pendryll, the vicar's wife started singing 'When Britain first, at heaven's command . . .' in this funny low voice.

As if entering the Ark, we filed carefully and awkwardly on to the shaky platform at the top of the field. The air was full of 'oohs' and 'aahs' and the clicking of cameras as parents suddenly recognised their offspring under all the Royal clobber. Mum waved at me from the front row, but King Alfred ignored her. Some distance away from the general crowd stood a small group of young men with cameras, and one pink fat bloke in naval uniform. Despite Badger's threats from the Kremlin the Russians had come.

The next thing I knew Arthur had mumbled his few verses, stepped back to scattered clapping and with a roll of drums it was Alfred's turn to tell them all about his cakes and heroic stand against the Vikings:

Against the fearsome sea-dogs of the North

We fought and . . . and . . . and saved our green land from the foe.

And he gave a wave with his wooden sword to show them he meant business.

So on it went with the others doing little tableaux things while the speaker trotted out his lines. Richard raised a cheer as he once more appealed in vain for his four-legged friend. Thornie's collie leapt on to the platform to offer his services, tail wagging, tongue out like a pink flag.

'I said "horse",' Chico growled loudly at him, patting his head to show that even Richard the Third could be kind to animals.

Elizabeth received gasps of admiration as she shouted her defiant lines over the school rooftops at the Welsh hills opposite. Towards the end of the long line you could see them getting restless and start to wander away. Then a wind sprang up again and blew away the last words of Queen Victoria. Finally, after the clapping at the end there was this long pause, with kings, queens and subjects all wondering what to do next. It was over, but it somehow seemed incomplete.

It was then that Thornie chose to drag the Russian skipper up on to the platform in front of us and point him at the crowd. Thornie explained to us how the ship was sailing in memory of a boat full of kids that sunk during the war, or something, and it was stopping at ports all over Europe.

The short bald figure looked round uneasily in front of the crowd as it shuffled back into place. Then he spoke — in English!

'Greetings to ze Breetish peepul from our country . . . mmm. It eez great honour end privelege . . . Senk-you-wery-much . . . And great honour and privelege to celebrate mmm . . .' He coughed and glanced nervously over to the distant group of sailors. 'To celebrate . . . the most magnificent event for the whole of mankind and after sixty-five years the bells of Red Square ring again for the freedom of all nations and senk-you-wery-much.'

Whatever he meant, I'm sure he meant well. Then he clambered uncertainly off the platform to polite applause and walked back to his little group. None of the sailors were clapping, but I suppose they couldn't understand English. The funny thing was that the Russians didn't walk round or speak to anybody, they just stood there by the science labs, far away from the rest of us, taking the occasional photo. Then they just wandered quietly off and left the pageant to its weary end.

By five o'clock it was all over. Badger congratulated us all and promised us a photo in the Gazette. Yet he seemed disappointed about something. Perhaps because all the glorious times he'd been on about were all in the past and all we had left were strikes, football hooligans, war films and Wimbledon.

Chico and I wandered sadly round the empty stalls for the last time. His parents hadn't turned up. But then his stepfather didn't think much of royalty, anyway. The air had cooled and the crepe paper rattled harshly in the breeze. The last shopkeeper, old Pinhead, was bawling 'Roll-up, roll-up' across the empty field, but not even Thornie's collie was interested any more. He'd had his day, getting his head patted by a Russian captain who could speak English.

Just as we were passing two teachers busy packing up a small tent we heard one say to the other, 'I suppose John's Royal Puppet Show was worth it.'

'I'm sure the mums and dads loved it,' the other grunted. 'Still, it keeps them off the streets.'

Chico frowned and gave me a nudge. 'Well I dunno about you, Alf, but I enjoyed meself even if no one else did, eh?' Then he added, 'What I don't get is why the Russians have been celebrating *our* Royal Family for the last sixty-five years.'

Before I could answer, who should swoop down behind us but Maria Kelly, actually smiling. 'Come on, kids, coming down our house? We're having a tea party. High society. Kings and queens only. Coming?'

And she wasn't joking either. Once we'd squeezed into their semi it was orange juice and rock cakes all round. She may not have been the perfect hostess, but her rock cakes certainly were fit for a king. Just as I reached out for the mouth-watering pile on the plate she slapped my hand.

'Not you, Alf! No, we got a special treat for you.' And her huge red-faced mother brought me in my cake on its own special plate. It was burnt and charred as black as a cannon ball.

I had to laugh — well, she might have hit me if I hadn't. And we all know how tough her ancestors were . . .

Lorenzo's Oracle

Life can be really down if you're a late developer at fourteen. It seemed as if all the boys and half the girls in our class were taller than me. All except Chico Marks (and we all know how he stunted his growth) and Mickey Lawrence, who even managed to be shorter. And he was skinnier and almost as brainy as me but not quite. It was good to have him around. He had a head like a lightbulb with a thin blue vein running down his face like some sort of filament, and two button-on eyes stuck on his front. His two buck teeth not only earned him a silly nick-name but gave him a slight lisp as well. So how could anybody have guessed that he was going to cause so much trouble?

Was the smallest, quietest boy in the class, sitting next to the biggest, Murphy, in tutor period, just about to start an arm wrestling match? At least Murphy had stuck out his huge paw and grunted; 'Come on then, Bugs, my turn.'

Murphy versus Mickey? Murphy, who could beat all the boys in the class and half the teachers as well? Even Braddock the sports teacher took five seconds to put him down.

I leaned forward for a closer look. But instead of gripping Mickey in the usual bone-crushing, flesh-pulping vice Murphy continued to hold his hand palm upwards. Mickey took it delicately by the finger tips.

'You'll have quite a long life . . . and . . . oh, and a stormy marriage,' he announced mysteriously. Murphy sat up, puzzled for a moment, then realising that at least he wasn't pronounced dead or diseased, he smiled bliss-fully.

Once word got round that Mickey had started foretell-ing the future everybody crowded round wanting to know what it had in store for them. By the time Stoney turned up to take the register there was a huge crowd of fortune hunters round the centre of the room. They all rushed to their seats except Chico, who was having his palm read.

Stoney didn't realise what was going on until Chico told him to wait because his fate was in the balance. Stoney, who hates any kind of back-chat, loomed over them.

'Does he read bumps?' he rumbled. Chico looked enquiringly at Mickey, then saw the clenched fist. He sagged with a groan as he understood this typical Stoney remark, and slid across to his place with arms raised.

Stoney was in a bad mood. It was two weeks before the summer fête and he now had the tedious task of drum-ming up enthusiasm and support. In other words, trying to get money out of us, or things that would get money out of others. This meant I would have to be nice to Dad and ask him to empty his pub for the bottle stall. To my amazement he didn't mind.

'Of course I don't mind!' he cheered heartily. 'Comprehensive education is not only good for social harmony — it's free as well.'

And he drank a quick toast from the whisky optic. I suppose because it was free that explained why we were always on the scrounge.

The minute Stoney found out that Mickey was 'into' fortune telling, as they say, he roped him in to the fête as a solo effort.

'What a flipping cheek!' Mickey lisped to us during the long trek to the science labs at the other end of school. 'He wants me to sit in this little tent and tell fortunes to all the mums and dads and that. Lorenzo's Oracle he's going to call it. What a waste of a Saturday afternoon!'

Chico's eyes lit up. He stopped and let the refugee train of kids and bags wind past him as he informed us of his brainwave.

' 'Ere, Bugs, ask to read old Pinhead's palm just before the end of lesson, then tell him he's going to have a car crash tonight. He might forget to set homework.

But Mickey wasn't that kind of trouble-maker, unfortunately. Actually, his parents had given him this book on fortune telling for his birthday and he'd spent the last three months understanding and memorising it. And, despite all the grumbles, Lorenzo's Oracle was there in his little green tent, opposite the china-smashing stall on that windy, changeable afternoon.

I was involved in some silly pageant that Badger had dreamt up to entertain the parents, so I had no idea how the Oracle was getting on. There was a question I would have dearly liked to ask, but I just didn't have the nerve to go and ask it. I mean we may all look forward to knowing our future, but what if our future's not worth looking forward to, if you know what I mean. Anyway, my fortunes had already taken a turn for the worse.

I had noticed this long queue of girls outside the tent, some of whom were in our class, but I thought nothing of it. Girls love that sort of thing. A crystal ball's almost as fascinating as a mirror, as far as they're concerned.

Monday morning, however, I was in for a shock. The instant I walked in through the classroom door I received a smacking great kiss on the mouth, a crushing embrace and had Maria Kelly cooing over me like a love-sick vulture.

'You do love me after all.'

'What? Who me? Gerroff!' I pleaded politely. She was taller than me and skinny; not exactly ugly but too much like a boy to be pretty. And she was as hard as nails. I was panic striken.

'I asked the Oracle on Saturday and what do you think he said? "Your wish to be granted." So I asked it again and it said — "He is your only true-love." '

Before she hauled me off for a quick kiss-and-cuddle over by the dustbins I managed to worm free and point the finger at Mickey.

'You swine! Why me? — I'll get you for this.'

He was more upset than scared. During the long trek to science that morning I caught up with him again and confronted him.

'You told that cow I was in love with her!' I accused.

'Of course I didn't. She picked the symbol, she asked the questions and all I did was tell her the answer out of the book. It's got nothing to do with me.'

I shouldered past him, mercilessly. He was getting on my nerves. I'd noticed something else too. Ever since he'd started this fortune-telling business he'd been surrounded by girls of all ages. By the end of the break he used to reek of perfume so much you'd think he was changing sex. They'd chase him all round the school just to have their palms read, or their fortunes told, or their moles analysed.

'Analysing moles, eh?' Chico murmured thoughtfully, in the library, 'I bet you get a few interesting revelations that way, eh?'

That library lesson we both had the same idea. I knew there was a book up there on palmistry, but so did Chico and he got it out first.

'You don't want that,' I snapped, snatching it from him. 'You wouldn't know what to do with it. Too many long words, anyway.'

'Mits off!' he hissed snatching it back. 'I know why you want it. 'Cos the quickest way to get the bird in the hand is to read her palm, right? Now, get lost!'

He paused and his eyes narrowed. 'Anyway, loverboy, what's the hurry? You're spoken for already aren't you? Going out with Maria Kelly, eh? You lucky boy.'

'That's not going out with — that's abduction!' I answered bitterly, and tried to get the book off him again. Not only did he keep it, he offered to hire it out to me for ten pence a day. That was the end of our friendship for the time being.

I sat in the corner of the library and watched him read the first few pages, close the book, close his eyes, try to memorise it, pick up the hand of the nearest girl — Lucy Gillimore, the swine — and start whispering. His eyes twinkled and widened, his smile grew, his teeth flashed. Her cheeks reddened. Her palm withdrew suddenly, then returned across his face, hard, twice.

I laughed so much I got a three-side essay from Mrs Potter. At dinner break, though, the laugh was on me. My troubles multiplied. I was playing tag with some of the lads when suddenly the game stopped. Three fourth year hardnuts stepped out of the toilets and marched towards me. When they had me caged in the corner, Burroughs stood on my foot, put his hands in his pockets and pretended to look harmless.

'So, you're the little runt who's going out with Kelly?' he growled. I nearly fainted. That was all I needed. Him jealous of me!

'Me? 'Course not.' I managed to whisper after three attempts.

'Oh no? I seen you round by the dustbins,' he told me, his hands out of his pockets now and holding my lapels under my cheek bone.

'I was k-kidnapped,' I protested. He considered this for a second, then gave a cunning grin.

'Oh yeah? Well in that case, I'm letting you go, aren't I? Oh, and if I catch you near her again . . . I'll hang you.'

Then, having left me in suspense, he slouched off across the yard to chat up Kelly herself. She treated him with total contempt, looked over his shoulder and beckoned wildly to me instead. It was all a plot. It had to be. I turned and ran.

I ended up seeking asylum in the poetry room and who

should be sitting at the table in the corner but Nostrada-
mus himself, chin on hand, staring emptily into space.

'Finished playing God, have you, you swine,' I sneered
at him. 'First Kelly tries to rape me because you said I
fancy her, then Burroughs tries to kill me cos he's jealous,
then Chico tries to chat up my . . . and it's all your fault!'

He didn't seem very interested. All he said was: 'Not
another one.' And he turned sadly away. 'First year girls
hate my guts because I told this girl her budgie would die,
and it did. Eight second year girls are broken-hearted
because I said their true loves were false. Now you.'

'Now me,' I repeated toughly. 'Because you're the little
trouble-maker, Bugs. Worse than that you're spoiling the
social harmony of our comprehensive school.'

'Me? I like that!' he squeaked angrily. 'All I do is read
the answers to their questions out of a book. How can
that be my fault? But oh no, everybody takes it personally. They think I'm *responsible* for their fate instead of just
prophesying it.'

He slumped back into his earlier depressed position. I
nearly felt sorry for the worm when something struck me
about what he'd just said.

'Prophesying?' I echoed slowly like he was something
out of the Old Testament. 'But you aren't a prophet, are
you?'

He shrugged and looked at me helplessly. 'Well, that's
the trouble. You lot seem to think I am, and so it amounts
to the same thing.'

Just then this nagging question, that I desperately
wanted answered came into my mind. Lucy Gillimore,
blonde, beautiful Lucy — the best dancer, the best actress

85

in the year. Even now she was in the other end of the pottery room, by the kiln, and she was coming over. Ignoring me, however, she started talking to Bugs. Would he read her fortune? Wearily, he dipped into his bag, pulled out the book and opened it at the page of symbols. She closed her eyes, waved her finger and came down on the black cat. I heard her ask the question: 'Is my true-love true?'

I stood behind her and nodded frantically. Lorenzo's Oracle replied.

'Your true-love is . . . false.'

She gave a funny gasp. I felt confused, but then relieved. Whoever he was he didn't deserve her. She turned and drifted past me dreamily, having second thoughts now, I hoped.

'Silly cow,' he jeered quietly after her. 'That's the fourth time this dinner hour. And a different answer each time.'

'Really?' I muttered, half to myself. 'Perhaps she's . . .'

I stopped myself just in time and swung round instead to look at the little clay models on the shelves. Funny thing, really; they call it a pottery lesson yet you hardly see any pots, let alone get a chance to make any. Instead you sit round the tables making models out of clay, like mucking about with plasticine. Most of the models were rubbish, hardly worth glazing, horses looking like elephants, dogs and cats looking like sheep. But then there was the occasional masterpiece by some kid who had magic at the end of his or her fingertips and could feel and mould things just the way they looked — like Lucy Gillimore's mare and foal, or goat, or an old man in a rocking chair. Each one was brilliantly true to life.

I wondered who this dreamboy was that she was moulding away in her delightful mind; the way I was trying to shape her out of my fantasies. Then there was Mickey, watching me closely now for some reason, the fortune teller who sort of moulded our futures with his palm reading and his oracles; shaping us by telling us how our futures were shaping up.

And that was why they taught pottery in school. Because that's all we are, bits of clay being moulded into shape by the teachers.

I was getting so carried away in my thoughts that Mickey passed his hand in front of me like I was blind, or daft. Then he looked at me suspiciously.

'You know something, Ducker? You're the only person in class who hasn't asked to have his fortune told,' he noted. 'Why's that, I wonder? Are you scared of something? Scared of me, are you?'

I pretended to laugh at this and remembered a saying of my grandmother.

'Who needs a fortune teller? What you are tomorrow . . . is what you do today,' I told him smugly. He wasn't impressed.

'Oh yeah, like an earthquake or a car crash or something?' he answered.

I felt like hitting him in his clever mouth for a moment, but there was a commotion on the steps outside the pottery room and I soon realised I wouldn't have to. Murphy and some of the lads, faces all pug-ugly with anger stormed in and surrounded him.

'You told Lorraine I was untrue,' he bellowed down at

our prophet, who gave a funny shiver. 'She won't even talk to me any more, thanks to you.'

The other lads growled mutinously. More kids crowded into the pottery room and added a couple of descriptions of extra domestic disasters to stir things up a bit more. All Mickey could do was throw his hands up to heaven, at the real culprit perhaps.

'Look,' he shouted, purple in the face. We all went quiet. 'All I do is say it will happen. That does not mean I want it to happen, or cause it to happen. Now why don't you dimboes understand that?'

I suddenly saw the answer to the problem, or at least the explanation. I flicked my fingers and pointed at him.

'You're luck! That's what it is. You are luck itself. If it's good luck we thank you for it, but if it's bad luck we can come along and give you a bloody good cussing for it. Get it?'

I looked round eagerly. Nobody got it.

'I mean for the first time we can actually get our own back on luck. Who do we blame normally if we get bad luck? No-one, right? Who do we blame now?'

Murphy stepped forward looking all thick and puzzled.

'Ah yeah, but you're forgetting one thing.' Then he paused. We waited to see what it was that I'd forgotten, but he couldn't remember.

'But what if it's some really bad luck?' Mickey wailed at me nervously.

I shrugged. 'That's . . . bad luck.'

Everybody laughed cruelly at him. The pottery room was full of kids now, even fourth years. I noticed Burroughs by the doors, but thankfully he had his arm round Maria Kelly, who was smiling for a change. Just then Chico burst through the crowd with a piece of paper in his hand. He sat down next to Mickey and grabbed his hand roughly.

'Your life line's shrinking fast. Bugs. Pick a symbol.'

On the piece of paper were some roughly drawn symbols — axes, knives, skulls, gallows and guillotines. Mickey closed his eyes, waved his finger round and came down on the gallows. Next he had to ask his question.

'Er . . . how do I get out of this mess?'

'Good question, Bugs. You promise never to bring your fortune telling book into school again, or read palms ever again, especially girls.'

He promised.

'Well, well, Mickey. Your future suddenly looks a lot rosier.'

They all congratulated him, laughing and patting his back and the bell went for afternoon registration. On the way out Mickey nudged Lucy Gillimore and jerked his thumb at me.

'By the way, Ducker fancies you like mad.'

'Does he?' all wide-eyed and blushing with amazement (at her good fortune) and burning passion. We both stood staring at each other while everybody rushed round us and the pottery room emptied.

Who needs fortune tellers, I thought? After all, like my grandmother used to say, 'What you do tomorrow . . . is what you are today.' Or something like that.

The Christmas Star

And yea it came to pass, that a great heap of little first years was gathered in the yard. And there was much babbling and laughter; and there was great joy indeed, as they tried to think up new ways of bankrupting their parents for Christmas. I felt quite sorry for adults suddenly; what with the price of petrol and taxation.

As for me, I'd seen it all before. I mean once you've got your bike, cassette recorder, camera and record player plus half a dozen of your favourite LPs, Christmas isn't what is used to be.

Just as the season of goodwill was beginning to go sour on me and I was starting to feel painfully grown-up myself, Chico Marks popped out of nowhere like a pantomine genie to brighten up Christmas for ever.

'I have had a real inspiration,' he announced with that famous baby-shark grin of his. He gazed at the first years while I asked what his inspiration was.

'How to raise funds for the Chico Marks Annual Orgy.'

'Raising funds?' I laughed. 'Who from? And how?'

'Would you believe — carol singing?' he told me and a couple of other fourth year lads who'd drifted towards us out of general boredom. We all jeered and laughed at this, until he produced a cassette recorder from out of his bag.

'All ready then?' he asked us and pressed the button. The tinsel tones of 'Silent Night' sang out at us for a few seconds. None of us was the wiser though. Stevie Brown stepped forward as it stopped.

'Ooh 'ere, I like that one. I like "Sky at Night".'

'Do you mind not interrupting me, dumbo?' Chico snapped as we all fell about laughing. He rolled his eyes at us and then put his arm round Stevie's shoulder.

'Look, er, Stephen. How d'you like to get in the Guinness Book of Records?'

Stevie's eyes lit up. He liked it, silently.

'Did you know that the record for running round the school is only twenty-nine? You can beat that, surely. Go on then!'

And off he went; running like a clockwork monkey. That was the last we'd seen of him that break. Then Chico continued to explain his fundraising plans.

'If "Top of the Pops" can do it, then why can't carol singers?' Chico asked pointing down at the cassette recorder, which he'd borrowed from the Music Department. He couldn't afford his own, yet.

'You know why carol singers earn chicken feed these days? It's because they're terrible. What we are going to do is mime, yes, mime to the professionals.' He stepped back and waited for us all to congratulate him.

I waited for a second, too, while a game of tag raced past us, then said, 'Oh sure, Chico. I mean, nobody will be able to tell the difference, will they? I mean when they see half a dozen scruffy yobboes, and hear the Vienna Boys Choir coming out of a cassette recorder, they aren't going to suspect anything, are they? Not much they won't.'

The other two nodded sarcastically and Chico got quite upset.

'That's nice, that is. Put the boot in before you even give it a go.' He was going quite red himself and started twitching his shoulders the way he does when he's being cussed by a teacher.

'All right,' he snapped. 'So make sure you only sing outside some old duck who's deaf as a post.'

'And how will they know we're singing then?' I asked laughing really loud. Then, I stopped abruptly. Up till then it had sounded like a pretty stupid idea. But as it happened there were quite a few old people living round our way in Swanswell village, nearly forty of them, and plenty of them seemed to be hard of hearing. It was almost worth giving it a go, just for a laugh.

The bell went and we all piled back into prison for Maths. Just as Stoney made his usual entry into the classroom — a single bellow and a clout or two — the grinning blond head of Stevie Brown bobbed past the window, ready for lap seven. The whole class followed his bobbing progress with amazement; including Stoney who leaned over by the window to reassure himself that what he had seen was true.

'What is he supposed to be doing?' he mused aloud.

'He's trying to get in the Guinness Book of Records, sir,' I told him, trying to keep a straight face. Stoney's face darkened with a deep rumble.

'Get him back in the building, will you,' he said to me.

Stevie might not have got into the Book of Records but he got in on the carol singing act, later that week. We chose Wednesday, three days before the end of term. It was the fourth year disco that same evening which meant that Chico, who lived miles away, could stay for tea at the pub, go carol singing later and perhaps spend some of the takings at the disco on coke and crisps.

It was a freezing cold night and every mutter of complaint and threat had its own little cloud of foreboding.

'This had better work,' puffed Murphy, having pulled the scarf off his mouth. He was big too, huge; so Chico had to reassure him fast.

'Relax, just don't forget to mime the words. And you, dimbo,' he turned to Stevie, 'you keep your mouth shut at all times, O.K.?'

'But 'ere I want to do singing,' he begged. Chico pulled Stevie's scarf back over his mouth. Nobody could figure out how Stevie came to be with us in the first place. Then we set to work.

Our first victim was old Mrs Cramphorn. She was eighty-seven, only half deaf and generally quite a nice old woman. We rang the bell, twice. Chico pressed the button, Kings College Cambridge started singing 'Silent Night', Stevie gave an opening squeak but was silenced by a couple of boots from the rest of the choir. We mimed for two verses, then the door opened and Mrs Cramphorn appeared like a Christmas ghost.

The singing stopped in the middle of 'heavenly peace' as Chico hid the cassette recorder behind his back and waited trembling for her verdict.

'Charming,' she said, clasping her hands together. 'Absolutely charming. I've never heard singing like it. Do please go on.'

'Thank you, madam,' stuttered Chico and then out of the corner of his mouth. 'This is going to be awkward. Er . . . we're such perfectionists, madam, we'll have to carry on exactly where we left off.'

And so we stood there, feeling complete chumps, miming to the music, sounding even worse from behind Chico's back, and waiting for her to realise she was being conned. But she didn't. We finished, she sang out her praises more than ever, thanked us warmly and gave us a pound. A real green note.

'There you are, you poor little boys. Now don't spend it all at once.'

Poor? Little? What with Murphy six foot tall and ugly with those gaps in his teeth? Chico all shifty-eyed, Stevie looking all blue-eyed and lost, and me a bag of nerves? Her eyesight must have been pretty far gone as well.

But as we stood admiring the loot a few yards down the road Murphy shuffled forward and turned the note over in his paw.

'A quid?' he growled uneasily. 'Eh, I reckon this isn't fair.'

'What are you on about fair?' Chico whined getting offended again. 'We'll split it four ways — what am I saying? Three and a half ways. Right? That's 33p each and a penny for Dumbo. What could be fairer than that?'

Murphy still shook his head. He squared up and towered over Chico menacingly.

'I don't reckon this be fair on the old dear,' he explained. 'I mean, you know, giving us a quid and all . . . what with her pension and everything.'

Chico shivered suddenly at the cold wind, or first hint of mutiny. Then it was his turn to explain patiently to Murphy that all was quite justified.

'Look, she liked it, didn't she? We performed a service, didn't we? You don't get anything for nothing these days, do you? What if we mimed it? So do people on telly and look how much they earn. Anyway what do I do? Knock on the door, give her the quid back and say, 'Happy Christmas, we were having you on!' Blimey, we could put her off Christmas for ever!'

The argument worked, for a while anyway. The pound disappeared into Chico's little box. But more problems were on their way. In the distance I had heard the sound of real carol singing and I realised the the local vicar was out and about with his usual flock of carol singers from church — the Authorised Version.

So we hurried on and must have visited twelve houses. We really did rake it in; mainly because they didn't get to the door till the first verse was over, and we made sure we didn't sing when anybody was watching us. But Stevie was getting very disconcerted.

'Here, this isn't any fun! When are we going to do singing then?'

Chico started hissing at him from the side of his mouth as another problem presented itself.

'Just keep your stupid mouth shut or . . . oh, hello Vicar. Happy Christmas to you and all that.'

The Reverend Pendryll stood gazing at us quizzically,

head on one side. He was looking at me, then at our money box. I strolled casually behind Chico to take the cassette recorder from his shaking hands. But the vicar suspected we were up to no good. Worse than that, he was quite friendly with my mum, a keen churchgoer.

'I hear you boys are giving us some competition,' he began, glasses twinkling. 'Carol singing, eh? Highly laudable. Tell me, what charity are you collecting for?'

I said Barnardos, Chico said Boys Club. Murphy said RSPCA and Stevie said: 'Eh? But I haven't done any singing yet.'

The Reverend Pendryll didn't seem to notice. He helped himself instead to our money box and when he opened it his eyes nearly mounted themselves on the lenses of his glasses. He was very impressed.

'You've made more money than we have!' he blurted out in jealous astonishment. Then he collected himself and put the money box behind his back. His glasses twinkled in the light of the street lamp. He suddenly looked very sinister for a vicar.

'But of course, boys, if you're collecting for three charities you'll need it. Tell me, boys . . . what's the secret of your success?'

While Chico and I thought up an answer, the rest of the official carol singers — adults most of them, Stoney's wife and the governors among them — gathered in a large crowd behind him, staring at us in cold curiosity.

'These boys are doing exceptionally well tonight,' the vicar told them. 'They must be something special. How would you like to give us a quick demonstration? Say, a quick verse of "Silent Night" perhaps?'

96

It may have been the coldest night for years, but we didn't notice. We had turned to stone already. That is all except Stevie . . .

'Eh? You want us to sing then? I been waiting all night to do singing.'

And before we could stop him, he stepped forward, cleared his throat and was off. You should have seen the vicar's face. All their faces were worth a photograph, come to think of it.

At first it was the look of astonishment, suspicious gloom and distaste that adults put on; then gradually they sort of grew out of it and lit up in slow surprise and finally delight. Chico gave me a nudge and I tried to look calmly indignant, because Stevie may have been the dumbest boy in the school but he had the most fantastic voice I'd ever heard. He just stood there and sang like a lark, a professional lark in fact. He sang so beautifully nobody seemed to notice that he was getting half the words wrong.

I could have kicked myself up a Christmas tree. All that messing about with cassette recorders and learning the words off by heart, and the miming, when all the time we had this priceless talent in our midst.

When Stevie finished, or rather when he stopped suddenly, saying; 'Ooh, sorry Vicar, but I don't know no more words, see.' They all rushed forward, clapping and laughing. Chico gave a rather loud sigh of relief.

'Blimey was that *clo-ose*!' and despite the sub-zero temperatures he tugged at his collar. 'I don't know about you, but I'm disco-bound.'

And without bothering to talk the vicar into parting

with his confiscated loot he walked quickly up the road to school, taking Murphy and the cassette recorder with him. Murphy was beaming all over his ugly face.

I still couldn't get over Stevie Brown and his Golden Voice. So I decided to stay around for a while and see what else was going on. Of course he was suddenly a star — a Christmas Star if you like. He and I walked back into town with the official carol singers and ended up singing carols in the market square, with Stevie right in the middle of the Christmas tree, singing 'Sky at Night' like an angel on leave, surrounded by voices and the cosy colours of Christmas, under the coal black, glinting sky.

The evening came to a halt at ten o'clock and everyone started to break up and go home to their hot punch and muffins. I went over to congratulate Stevie personally. He'd had so many pats on the head that night that he had a sort of happy stunned look about him.

Suddenly a dirty old car pulls up at the kerb and this huge drunk staggers out and lurches towards our Christmas angel.

'An' where the bloody 'ell 'ave you been all night?' this voice roared. Everybody turned round. It was his dad.

'I bin doing singing,' Stevie peeped, like a young bird before a huge hungry wolf.

'Singing? I'll give you singing! We been worried sick about you!'

Stevie had gone out without telling anybody. But I somehow doubted if old Brown was as worried as all that. He just liked a good row. Luckily the vicar was near at hand, and he hurried over to the rescue.

'He's been helping the choir, Mr Brown,' he explained

kindly, but firmly. 'Did you know your son has a beauti-ful soprano voice?'

Brown took his cap off for some reason and gaped down at his offspring who gaped back up at him, waiting.

''Ave 'ee?' said Brown. 'Well I never knew that. Well I'll be damned!'

'Come now, Mr Brown,' said the vicar. 'Let's not jump the gun, shall we?' And he ushered the bewildered drunk back into his car. Stevie was allowed to stay behind for his fair share of punch and hot muffins.

Once the news that Stevie could sing got round to Thornie, our headmaster, he was instantly lumbered with a solo in the School Carol Service at the very end of term. Not that I had anything to laugh at. I had to read the lesson straight after him!

I sat there shivering in the pew as Stevie stood up straight and still with that happy-bewildered look on his face. And he sang:

'One sing Roy all day vidsitee . . .'

I could see all the kids and all the teachers glancing round at each other in surprise and disbelief as our Christmas Star sparkled for us. Then it was my turn. I felt dreadful. The words of the Bible swam before me.

But then I thought, if Stevie can do it, then I can do it as well.

The microphone crackled ominously and I could hear my voice boom back at me from the ancient pillars and walls:

'And it came to pass in those days, that there went out a decree from Caesar Augustus that all the world should be taxed . . .'

GRYPHON BOOKS

Some other series titles you may like to read are described in the following pages.

A NASTY PIECE OF WORK

by Lance Salway

A new supermarket which has replaced an old-fashioned grocer's is plagued by mysterious happenings – who does the voice over the tannoy belong to?

Plates fly across the room and are smashed in a large family home – what is going on?

A girl with none of her twin sister's talent for singing and dancing suddenly gains it – but where from?

A boy ridicules a classmate's talk of magic, yet has a shocking experience himself . . .

In these scary stories Lance Salway writes about ordinary girls and boys – and the *extra*ordinary things that can happen to them when the 'ghosties and ghoulies' take over. The most innocent situations become sinister, the most normal turn nasty. Fortunately there's comedy too: some of the ghosts have a sense of humour!

2
THE RETURN OF THE *ANTELOPE*

by Willis Hall

For Gerald and Philippa Gartstanton, their 1899 summer holiday isn't proving much fun. They have a dragon of a seaside landlady and even their nice grandfather wants them to spend far too much time modelling for his new-fangled photography. But everything changes for the better when the children find themselves caught up in the return of the *Antelope*.

Exactly two hundred years earlier, a ship called the *Antelope* had carried Gulliver on his travels to the miniature state of Lilliput. Now Gerald finds on the beach a tiny but perfect replica of the *Antelope*, and three remarkable little people enter the children's lives.

Willis Hall's delightful novel is based on the series he wrote for Granada Television.

4
THE HOUSE OF
SIXTY FATHERS

by Meindert DeJong

'And then will come a day when there will be
no more shooting, and no more running from
the shooting, and no war. There will come a
day when the little family of Tien will go back
to their little village, and live in peace.'

But can this ever be? For this is the Second
World War in China. The Tiens' village has
been burned and they have been driven far
from it by the Japanese invaders. Worse still,
the family has been split up. Young Tien Pao,
sleeping one day in the sampan, has woken up
to find that the moorings have broken and he
has drifted back into Japanese-held territory.
With only the squealing family piglet for
company, Tien Pao must attempt a long and
dangerous journey.

This is the classic story of a child in wartime. It
tells how Tien Pao reaches the House of Sixty
Fathers, and keeps alive the hope of seeing his
family again.

9
NO PLACE LIKE

by Gene Kemp

It's hard to be 16 and an academic failure in the Williams household. Pete's big sister Sal is confident and brilliant. His Dad's sarcastic in a long-suffering way. His Mum's into CND and sociology: Pete only scrapes into the Sixth Form College because she knows old Weevil Bird, the principal. It's not the best start for Pete to tread on Weevil Bird's glasses – or to set fire to the waste bin in the coffee bar, or partially blow up the chemistry lab.

But if Pete is accident prone, he's a survivor, and a thoroughly likeable character. It's Pete who sees the danger when his progressive Mum has two unsavoury youths to stay. And when he meets the 'cobweb girl' he has glimpsed and dreamt about, he's determined to be Cagney, Bogart and Napoleon rolled into one!

'A home-and-school teenage novel which is at once brisk, incisive, perceptive, gloriously funny and – dare I say it – kind . . . Not to be missed'.
Naomi Lewis in the *Listener*.

DEVIL ON MY BACK

by Monica Hughes

Tomi Bentt has done well in the underground world of ArcOne. In this 22nd century city, Lords, soldiers, workers and slaves all have their place in a totally controlled environment. Tomi is a Young Lord, and will become one of the rulers of the city if he can access all the heavy infopacks plugged into the back of his neck.

But a mishap forces Tomi out into the world beyond ArcOne, where it seems that only savages now survive. His infopacks are useless here: he needs older human skills, and must develop parts of himself that no computer has programmed. In time he even discovers the truth about ArcOne, and contemplates an awesome project . . .

Monica Hughes writes science fiction with strong human interest. This is a richly imagined story of great power.